'Not much of a holiday so far,' Josh murmured.

'You've been in the wrong place at the wrong time twice today.'

'Or in the right place,' Bethan countered. 'It depends on your point of view.'

He smiled wanly and closed his eyes, and Bethan's heart clenched in sympathy when she suddenly realised that it wasn't just the effccts of his injuries which were giving him such a drawn appearance. Now that the pain-killing drug was forcing him to relax, she could see that the man looked absolutely exhausted.

Dear Reader

I am lucky enough to live in one of the most beautiful parts of Britain—right on the border between Devon and Cornwall and within minutes of some of the most unspoilt scenery you could hope to find.

Every mile of open moorland and granite tor, every twisting lane and secret cove is full of history, mystery and hidden romance.

When I was asked if I would like to write a story about someone whose much needed break from work unexpectedly turns into a 'busman's holiday', where else could I set it but here?

My heroine, Bethan, came to Cornwall to find the peace and space she needed to decide on a new direction for her life. It was sheer chance that brought her into contact with local GP Joshua and his daughter Sam. She couldn't have foreseen that fate would bring them together again just a few hours later, nor the effect they would have on each other's hearts.

I hope you enjoy their story and that one day you have the chance to visit the beautiful part of the country where it happened.

Happy reading,

Josie

PROMISES TO KEEP

BY
JOSIE METCALFE

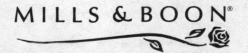

All the characters in this book have no existence outside the imagination of the author, and have no relation whatsoever to anyone bearing the same name or names. They are not even distantly inspired by any individual known or unknown to the author, and all the incidents are pure invention.

*First published in Great Britain 1998
Harlequin Mills & Boon Limited,
Eton House, 18-24 Paradise Road, Richmond, Surrey TW9 1SR*

© Josie Metcalfe 1998

ISBN 0 263 81073 9

*Set in Times Roman 11 on 11½ pt.
03-9808-50534-D*

*Printed and bound in Norway
by AiT Trondheim AS, Trondheim*

CHAPTER ONE

'PLEASE, Daddy! Not yet!' begged the little voice behind Bethan, its childish tones reaching her clearly in spite of the surrounding frantic gaiety as she sidestepped a huge bunch of multicoloured balloons. 'Can't we stay just a *little* bit longer?'

'Sam,' said a patient baritone. 'It's already long past your bedtime.'

'But, Daddy, it'll be a whole *year* before the fair comes back again...'

Bethan couldn't help smiling at the tone of the words, uttered as desperately as if a year were half a lifetime away.

She glanced over her shoulder towards the wheedling child, unsurprised to see that the youngster was firmly ensconced on a broad pair of shoulders.

And they *were* broad shoulders, in keeping with their owner's six-feet-plus in height and clothed in a deep sky-blue T-shirt which had probably started the afternoon pristine but was now smudged with grass-green smears where a pair of diminutive trainers dangled.

She felt her smile broaden as she watched skinny arms wrap themselves around the lean planes of the man's angular chin and squeeze, the child's short dark curly hair mingling with his as a sticky-looking cheek was laid on top of his head.

'Just *one* more ride down the twisty tower thing?' The bargaining continued hopefully, deep blue eyes peering down now into their adult double. 'Then we can go straight home.'

'That's what you said an hour ago, monster,' he grumbled, and Bethan could tell from the resignation in his tone that the child had won—again.

For one brief moment her eyes met the deep blue gleam of his and she could see the mixture of exasperation and love which filled them before he included her briefly in their tight family circle with a roll of his eyes and a comical grimace.

She couldn't help the grin that curved her lips in response, suddenly aware of his striking good looks as he smiled up at his child and smoothed one hand over tousled dark curls.

The fatherly gesture was so openly loving that, for a split second, she was struck by a shaft of...what? Envy? Regret?

The crowd shifted around them and the two of them were quickly swallowed up as they began to make their way towards the 'twisty tower thing' but the memory of the heart-warming picture they'd made stayed with Bethan as she continued to wander around the fair-cum-agricultural-show.

She hadn't expected to find anything like this going on when she'd booked her last-minute holiday—hadn't even been expecting to take a break this month at all until she'd found out the *real* reason Simon had wanted her to swap holiday dates...

As it was, the last couple of days had been deadly quiet as she'd wandered aimlessly through the picturesque towns and villages of this part of Cornwall, wondering what on earth had possessed her to come here. It was hardly the usual holiday destination for a woman on her own—far more suitable for families or honeymooners than someone with too much on her mind and too many empty hours to think about it.

She'd thought about joining the multitudes on their exodus towards exotic destinations, but in the end had decided that there wasn't much point in wasting so much money just to make a point. It wasn't as if Simon really cared where she was going, not once she confronted him with the fact that she'd found out that he was trying to arrange to go away with someone else.

No, what she really needed was to sort her life out, and Cornwall, basking in an early August heat wave, had seemed as good a place as any to do it.

Then, just an hour ago, she'd been idly driving around, exploring some of the more outlandish-sounding villages, when she'd seen the posters for the fair.

Something had prompted her to follow the signs which had led her to joining the serried ranks of vehicles, parked in an adjoining field, and thence towards the cheerful cacophony of the gathered crowds.

Several times she thought she caught a glimpse of the same tall dark-haired man, carefully lifting his child onto one of the brightly coloured fairground attractions, but it was never him.

It was some while later that she found herself standing near the brightly painted helter-skelter, watching each customer come screaming down the spiral to land in a laughing heap on the pile of mats at the bottom.

The air was full of exciting sounds and scents—loud music and the cheerful voices of people enjoying themselves while they sampled the hot dogs and burgers, sizzling at stands dotted along the way, or indulged in the empty calories of sticky pink candyfloss.

Suddenly, she realised that once more her eyes were scanning each new face as they swept into view on the 'twisty tower thing', looking for the man and his precocious child.

'Oh, for heaven's sake!' she muttered on an exasperated breath, and shook her head at her own stupidity as she turned away.

She'd thought that this time away from the hospital would help her to rationalise her bitter disappointment over the end of her rosy dreams of a family of her own. If the way she was mooning after the handsome stranger and his child was anything to go by she had some way to go yet... And she hadn't even started to sort out her options for the next step in her career...

Just the thought was enough to bring back the despondency which had been plaguing her for days.

With her enjoyment of the afternoon rapidly fading into oblivion, she made her way towards the exit, barely bothering to glance into the marquees full of prize-winning exhibits for baking and arts and crafts of every description.

Bethan glanced briefly to one side and, over the heads of the encircling crowd, saw a show ring full of cattle. The fact that each beast was proudly sporting a fluttering rosette told her that this must be some sort of victory parade.

She'd already watched a troupe of baton-twirling majorettes, warming up ready to follow the band around the flag-draped enclosure for their own lap of honour, but her enthusiasm for watching was gone.

With a deep sigh she turned away and began to walk towards the field full of cars.

The sun was deliciously warm but Bethan grimaced when she thought how long her little compact had been sitting closed up. It was going to be like climbing into an oven when she got into it.

Since she'd arrived at the show she'd been wearing a light cotton shirt draped over her shoulders so that she wouldn't get burnt. Now she slipped it off and folded it over her arm, leaving just her silky vest-style camisole on for comfort. Even that was probably going to be too warm, but she could hardly drive around in her bra—pretty as it was.

She was just fumbling in the bottom of her bag to find the keys to her car when, over the general cacophony, she heard the abrupt drumroll and trumpet fanfare that signalled the striking up of the band.

Just seconds later the air was split by a scream which froze her blood, the terror-filled sound travelling clearly over the triumphant opening notes of the victory march.

Without a second thought she whirled back towards the sound, her Accident and Emergency training kicking in as she began to run back towards the sound, guided by a growing chorus of further shrieks and shouts.

Soon she was met by the sight of tightly packed spectators, scrambling and pushing at each other to get away from the ringside.

For a moment she had to battle against the tide of humanity as people fought frantically to evade some unknown danger, their faces frozen in terror as they abandoned belongings in a scattered trail in their wake.

Some were going over like skittles and Bethan spared a thought for the number of injuries there would be by the end of the episode.

Suddenly the crowd parted, and for the first time

Bethan caught sight of the terrified young bull which was the cause of the turmoil.

Time slowed to a crawl and she seemed to be trying to run through treacle as she tried to absorb every detail.

In the blink of an eye she saw the way the sun shone off the animal's polished black hide as he darted towards the place where the crowd was thinnest.

The single cable, marking the ringside, was a puny barrier against his weight and terror, but once past that obstacle he seemed to be making towards the open space between the show ring and the small funfair.

All would probably have been well if some misguided person hadn't flapped their arms at him and sent him off in the wrong direction—back towards the milling crowd.

Ring stewards were still giving chase, but the gleaming white leading rope dangled out of reach between lethally sharp hooves, the heavy head swinging from side to side as the bull tried to find a way through the fleeing humans.

Suddenly, a dark-haired youngster stumbled into the path of the thundering hooves and Bethan didn't need any more than a blink of an eye to recognise the curly hair and the denim dungarees.

'Sam!' she breathed in horror.

She tried to force her feet to greater speed but she knew that no matter how fast she ran she could never get there in time. The fear-crazed bull would reach the child long before she could.

Without conscious thought she changed her angle of approach and headed straight for the solid body and lethal hooves, registering with a sinking heart that his pace had increased as a clear path opened up in front of him.

At the last moment she saw strong, masculine arms reaching out to sweep Sam to safety, then there was no time for Bethan to register anything other than the fact that the beast had veered towards her—the last obstacle between himself and freedom.

Instantly her concentration sharpened, her focus centred on the danger approaching on thundering hooves. Without having to think about it, she shook out the folds of the shirt still clutched in one hand, her attention never leaving the wildly rolling eyes of the crazed beast.

She was hardly aware of anything around her as she focused on the all-important timing, totally ignoring the hands which would have pulled her to safety as she swept her hands up and out to leave her shirt draped over the brutish bulk of the creature's head, only just remembering in time to step aside.

Everything would have worked perfectly if she had only remembered that the surface underfoot was a rough-mown meadow. As it was, one lightweight summer sandal caught against a tussock of grass and threw her off balance.

Before she could do anything about it she felt herself falling and, with the mental image of those lethal hooves flashing through her mind, closed her eyes and sent up a despairing prayer as she waited for the impact...but the only impact she felt was her own on the ground.

For a moment she didn't know whether the pounding she could hear was the animal's hooves or her own racing heartbeat.

Cautiously she opened her eyes and stared up at the eggshell blue dome of the sky, with not a cloud in sight on this perfect summer day. Slowly she became aware that the band had descended through cacophony to silence, and it was only when she heard the sound of someone moaning nearby that she began to realise that the danger might be over.

'Well done, maid,' said an admiring voice just behind her, his accent as broad as anything she'd heard since she'd arrived in Cornwall.

'Grab the rope, someone,' called another voice. 'Quick, before it takes off again...'

Sound broke over her in a wave as life started again, and she managed to get one elbow under herself to help her to sit up.

'Are you all right?' demanded a husky baritone, as a strong arm circled her shoulders to steady her.

'I'm fine,' she said slightly breathlessly as she looked up into a familiar pair of dark blue eyes.

'Are you sure?' This time he put a solicitous hand under her elbow to help her to her feet. 'You went down with quite a thump.'

'I'll probably have a bruise or two to take home as a souvenir, but otherwise... How's Sam? Did you get there in time?'

She looked around but couldn't immediately see the youngster.

'Sam's fine,' he reassured her with a smile. 'Thanks to your quick thinking. I presume you've had extensive training as a bullfighter?'

Bethan thought of the bedlam which often ensued in the A and E department on a Friday night. She'd discovered very quickly that she'd have to be able to think on her feet to avoid becoming one of the victims of mindless drunken violence.

'Something like that,' she confirmed with a wry

smile. 'At any rate, I've had some practice at avoiding antisocial animals…'

She was distracted by the sound of someone groaning nearby and suddenly realised that here she was smiling and exchanging cryptic comments while she was surrounded by injured people. The second realisation was that she had years of medical training in her head and nothing more than her hands to help her deliver the care.

'Look, do you know if someone will have phoned for some sort of assistance for the people who were hurt, or is there a first-aid station on the showground?' she asked, worried that no one seemed to be doing much to help.

'Yes, to both,' he confirmed as he straightened and began to turn away. 'I just had to make certain you hadn't been injured, helping Sam, but now I'd better get to work…'

With a last distracted smile in her direction he was striding away, his long powerful legs easily eating up the distance as he made his way swiftly towards the trail of destruction the frightened animal had left in his wake.

If she hadn't been watching him, her eyes following his broad shoulders into the crowd, she wouldn't have seen the way people seemed to make way automatically for him, nor would she have realised that they were speaking to him when they were calling for the doctor to help them.

She hesitated for a moment, wanting to offer her help but knowing that there was nothing worse than someone barging in where they weren't needed.

In the event, even with medically trained volunteers from the crowd helping the staff from the first-aid station, there were so many people needing attention that she realised her help *would* be welcome.

'Have you got some gloves?' she asked the uni-
formed nurse quietly when it seemed as if she could
do with at least another two pairs of hands. She would
hardly have been expecting this number of casualties
when she'd started her shift at the first-aid station.

'I *am* a medic,' Bethan confirmed, when a neatly
shaped eyebrow curved sharply. 'I'm on holiday from
my A and E job upcountry.'

She mentioned the hospital and found to their mu-
tual delight that they'd both trained at the same place.

'I'm Jane Trethorne and I'm delighted to meet
you—in spite of the fact that this seems to be turning
out to be a bit of a busman's holiday for you.'

'Bethan Mallory—and I'd rather be making myself
useful like this than baking on a beach any day!'

'Glutton for punishment!' Jane teased as she provided the gloves and they set to work.

For the next half-hour they interspersed the examination and treatment of each injury with conversation
about familiar places and people from their student
days.

Bethan found it amazing how much they had in
common even though they'd never worked together
before.

Their tongues were only stilled temporarily when
she had to concentrate on the essential task of distracting a young child while her broken arm was supported in a sling for the journey to hospital.

'All right, sweetheart?' Bethan said gently. She
didn't need to touch the arm the child was clutching
protectively against her to find out what was wrong.
The displacement of the broken ends of the bones just

above her wrist was obvious even through the spreading bruise.

'I need someone clever to help me do the doctoring. Are you going to help me?' Bethan asked with a coaxing smile.

'H-how?' whispered the tearstained moppet, her little chin wobbling as she gazed up, obviously fearful of what was going to happen to her.

She was trying hard to be brave, but she couldn't have been more than four or five years old—about the same age as Sam. But this wasn't the time to be thinking about the doctor's child. She had this little girl relying on her concentration and expertise.

'I need you to hold onto your arm to keep it nice and still, and hold the corner of this for me at the same time,' Bethan said, holding up one point of a triangular sling.

The youngster looked down at her misshapen arm cradled in her other hand and looked back up at Bethan, her forehead furrowed in a frown.

'How?' she demanded, her voice much stronger now that she was concentrating on something other than her pain. 'I got no more hands.'

'And your feet are too far away,' Bethan added with a pretence at seriousness. 'Well, if your hands are already busy, and your feet are too far away, then it'll have to be your teeth,' she said, offering the fabric.

The child was obviously intrigued now, and closed her small white teeth willingly over the offered corner.

'Right, now,' Bethan continued, glancing up towards the child's hovering mother. 'What we have to do is ask your mum to see if she can count up to ten before I can finish putting your hurt arm to bed. Are we all ready? Get set, go!'

With the swift expertise of long practice, Bethan wound the fabric around the back of the slender neck and down over the injured arm, camouflaging the fact that she was going to have to slide the other corner underneath the injured arm.

By the time the young woman had reached the end of her count, Bethan had settled the arm into position in the sling and was ready to tie the two ends into a knot.

'Right, sweetheart, if you can let me have that corner back, shall I turn it into a butterfly's wings?'

She swiftly tied the ends into a flat knot and fluffed the corners into perky 'wings' to decorate one shoulder, then tidied and secured the corner around the child's grubby elbow with a strip of adhesive tape.

'There you are. Easy! And now you're all ready to go for a ride to have a picture taken of your arm.'

Bethan found herself smoothing the child's baby-fine hair away from the 'butterfly' she'd fashioned, and had to force herself to concentrate on saying her goodbyes to the grateful mother and directing her towards the waiting ambulance.

What on earth was the matter with her today? she thought as she watched the young mother shepherd her little girl away. Why did she suddenly seem to be so susceptible to these youngsters? It wasn't as if she didn't see children just like them time and again every day...

Jane Trethorne's voice interrupted her thoughts and it was time to attend to the next person, waiting for attention.

This time it was a fairly nasty gash along a young farmer's temple, which needed cleaning and a liberal application of steri-strips before it would stop bleeding.

He was a big brawny chap, his muscles obviously the result of many hours of hard physical labour rather then a high-tech machine in some yuppie gym, but Bethan soon learned that he wasn't nearly as tough as he looked. She had hardly started talking about the fact that he looked as if he needed stitches before he had backed off with a look of panic in his eyes.

'Can't you just stick it together with that stuff like strips of Sellotape?' he said with a touch of desperation in his voice. 'I don't mind 'jecting the beasts when they need it, but I can't abide needles anywhere near me.'

Bethan and Jane exchanged a secret grin when she had to agree to do her best, without using any needles. Jane set about distracting their unexpectedly squeamish patient from what they were doing by asking how he'd received his injury.

'Frickin' 'orse kicked me,' muttered the burly young man, his face quite green in spite of his late-summer leathery tan. 'Damn band set all the beasts off with banging that frickin' drum.'

'Is that what made the bull panic?' Jane questioned as she cleaned some of the blood off his face and neck to make him look a little more presentable. There wasn't much she could do for the gory state of his clothing.

'Would have been all right if they'd just had the majorettes, same as they do every year,' he grumbled, as he gingerly held his blood-soaked handkerchief between finger and thumb as if he wasn't quite sure what to do with it. 'But this time the committee decided to make a big "do" of it, with the band leading the winners around. Waste of time and money, if you ask me—specially when you get prize animals scattin' about all over the place…could do themselves a damage.'

Bethan offered to dispose of the ruined handkerchief for him and he gratefully dropped it into the bag she proffered, before disappearing across the showground to get back to his animals.

'The speed he's going you'd think he's afraid that you'll change your mind and insist on using stitches,' Jane said with a chuckle. 'Although how he thinks either of us would be able to hold him down to do it, I don't know. He must weigh as much as the two of us put together!'

A little while later Bethan was crouching down beside a tearful elderly lady.

'I only went to pick up my grandson and something went snick inside,' she explained in a trembling voice. 'My daughter was married for twenty-three years before she fell pregnant with 'im. 'E's so precious to us and I was so afraid 'e was going to get trampled, and I end up falling on 'im.'

'Well, he's been checked over and he's perfectly all right,' Bethan reassured her gently. 'Now, all we've got to do is get a picture taken of this ankle of yours so we can find out if you've done *yourself* any damage.'

''E's gone a very funny colour and 'tis all swelling up,' the poor soul whispered as she gazed down at her ankle in horror. 'How'm I going to help Father do the milking if I can't put 'im to the ground?'

The woman's strapping great son-in-law had just arrived on the scene and was quick to tell her that there would be no problem with her cows.

'Don't you fret, Mother,' he said matter-of-factly. 'If Father can't manage I can send over my cowman or, better still, I can come over myself—long as you've got a bite of saffron cake I can have afterwards!'

Bethan couldn't help smiling at the way the burly man treated his mother-in-law.

The phrase 'bull in a china shop' leapt to mind when she saw the way his large hands dwarfed the handles on the borrowed wheelchair, but when she saw how carefully he pushed the fragile woman across the grass she could see the other side of him. Her opinion was confirmed when he lifted the elderly lady in his arms to help her into the front seat of his car to start the journey to the accident centre.

Gradually the queue dwindled until there was just the usual summertime trickle of sunburn, dehydration and wasp stings to cope with.

Bethan straightened up and stripped off her gloves, realising almost regretfully that her usefulness was at an end.

All the time she'd been working her eyes had kept straying towards the broad back of the man similarly occupied at the other end of the impromptu casualty station.

Occasionally she'd heard his deep voice, murmuring to a patient or to their shocked relatives, but he'd been just too far away for her to decipher the words.

Once she'd actually met his deep blue gaze, and when he'd smiled at her had given him an answering nod. She'd been surprised to feel her heart give a silly little skip, and she'd had to drag her gaze away when she'd felt a wash of heat drift over her face.

Now the emergency was over they wouldn't be needing any extra volunteers and she would have no reason to hang around. She snorted quietly as the little voice of honesty spoke in her ear.

What she really meant was that she didn't have an excuse any more for standing around and ogling the good-looking doctor.

It would just serve her right if his wife came over to collect him and he ended up introducing them...

She looked around for her bag and spied it tucked under the chair with several others, but there was no sign of the shirt she'd used as an impromptu toreador's cape.

'I suppose it's time I made my way to my car,' she began, then offered her hand to Jane. 'It was lovely meeting you, even if it wasn't under terribly auspicious circumstances.'

'Well, at least you know the natives are friendly in this part of the country,' Jane quipped, then added in a persuasive tone, 'You wouldn't fancy meeting up for a drink, would you? There's a group of us going out on Friday evening—all of us connected with medicine in some form or another—and it's a bit of a chance to let our hair down and talk shop at the same time.'

Bethan was tempted.

Her holiday so far had been so terribly solitary, and while she'd needed the time to do some serious thinking she was beginning to wonder if she would drive herself mad before she came to any decisions.

'Where are you going to meet up?' she asked, feeling her spirits beginning to lift already.

'Jamaica Inn,' Jane said with a grimace.

'Why the face?' Bethan was taken aback. 'Isn't that the place that Daphne du Maurier's famous book is named after?'

'It *was*,' Jane said significantly. 'Unfortunately, it's become rather over-commercialised to cater for sight-seeing tourists, but when you sit at one of the outside tables you're totally surrounded by some of the best views of Bodmin moor you'll ever see.'

Bethan was so tempted by the prospect of some congenial company that she was ready to leap at the invitation.

It was only the thought that her loneliness might seem horribly over-eager that made her opt for nonchalance, and Jane had to be content with a promise that she would try to be there.

Bethan smiled at her new friend and turned away, not to go towards her car but to make her way across to a certain tall dark and handsome doctor to introduce herself properly.

Her heart was fluttering in her chest like a trapped bird, and the smile she pinned to her face felt distinctly false as she tried to think of something intelligent to say.

She could have saved herself the bother because he wasn't there.

Bethan blinked in disbelief, her eyes flicking from side to side in search of him in case he'd just stepped away for a minute to talk to someone, but he'd disappeared.

Her heart sank and she sighed as she gave a wry shrug.

If she was brutally honest with herself there hadn't really been any point in speaking to the man, other than to get another look at him. He really was a rather gorgeous specimen, but just the fact that he'd had young Sam with him was enough to tell her that he was already taken.

That was enough to activate the rigorous ethics instilled in her by her grandmother. Unlike some women she could think of, she wasn't interested in breaking up other people's relationships, no matter how attractive she found a man...

Although the afternoon was drawing to a close, it was still too early to go back to her hotel, comfortable though it was.

The heat had gone out of the sun now, and a scattering of clouds along the horizon foretold a beautiful sunset. The trouble was, she didn't feel in the right frame of mind to enjoy it by herself.

A pair of dark blue eyes superimposed themselves onto her thoughts and she tried vainly to stop herself picturing the rest of the man that went with them—even trying to force herself to substitute little Sam's engaging face instead—but it didn't work.

Bethan sighed and pulled the car over into a designated parking area which gave her an almost panoramic view of miles of undulating moorland, each tor topped by its own rugged granite outcropping.

'It's time to put the whole thing in perspective,' she said aloud, quite forgetting that she'd wound the window down until she saw the way her voice startled an innocently grazing sheep.

'It's my biological clock,' she continued with a mental apology to the sheep, which was glaring at her from a safe distance. 'I had already started thinking about getting married and starting a family, and now I can't stop the damn thing ticking.'

She listened to the wind, soughing through the tall dried stalks of the moorland grasses, and grimaced when she heard the words for the lies they were.

Oh, there was an element of truth in them... She had, after all, been expecting to marry Simon, in spite of the fact that her grandmother's upbringing wouldn't allow her to agree to go away on holiday

with him. And with her rather old-fashioned background, there was no way that marriage could mean
anything other than a lifetime of love and fidelity and
children...

She'd been perfectly willing to do her colleague a
favour and swap holiday dates...until she'd found out
that the last-minute substitution was specifically for
Simon's benefit so that he could go away for his fortnight in the sun with another, far more accommodat-
ing woman.

She drew her thoughts up short.

There was no point in wallowing over all that she'd
lost when she'd found out that Simon didn't share her
expectations.

What did concern her now was the way she'd become fixated on the first good-looking man she'd
bumped into, regardless of the fact that he was obviously a happy family man.

By now he was probably at home with that family,
getting ready to spend the rest of this lovely August
evening together.

Perhaps it was his job to give their child a bath
while his wife made them some supper. Then, after
the little one was in bed, he would help her to clear
away the dishes and they would curl up together on
the settee and...

'Oh, what do *you* know about it?' she demanded
impatiently, remembering just in time to keep her
voice down so that she didn't scare the animals again.

This time it was a moorland pony that had wandered close to the car, her foal beside her just a few
months old and already starting to learn how to cope
with the tough moorland grasses he would have to eat
if he was to survive his first winter.

'Babies everywhere!' Bethany muttered crossly, refusing to allow herself to be charmed by his knobbly knees and bottlebrush tail. 'And after the fiasco with Simon, instead of swearing off men entirely or being on the lookout for someone eligible, what do I do...?'

She didn't need to finish *that* sentence aloud as she reached for the keys again, having to content herself with a dull aching envy for the unknown woman.

She'd turned the car round and was making her way back in the general direction of her hotel when a stray thought occurred to her.

Jane Trethorne had seemed to know who her mystery doctor was, although she hadn't mentioned his name. If she *did* decide to join Jane and her friends for that drink at Jamaica Inn, there was a very good chance that someone in the group would say something which would give her the opening to ask who he was.

Perhaps when he lost his air of mystery she would be able to forget him.

She was smiling at the thought as she came upon yet another crossroads, each arm of the signpost adorned with yet another selection of typically Cornish names.

She'd noticed immediately just how many of them started with Tre, Pol and Pen, and as she peered upwards she realised that these were no exception.

'Tresillet and Pendruccombe,' she read aloud, loving the strange rhythm to them.

A quick glance at the little clock on the dashboard told her she still had plenty of time to explore, and the name Pendruccombe seemed to be calling to her.

She set off down the road, marvelling that it was hardly wider than a lane with the solid Cornish 'hedges' of stacked granite on either side of her.

Every so often she would top a rise and catch a

glimpse of distant vistas, with a square church tower emerging through a full-leaved canopy to show where the village lay huddled in the valley.

It was all so delightful, from the fresh, sun-warmed breeze teasing her hair as it flowed in through her open window to the stately spires of foxgloves rooted between every other stone.

The sign for a ford caught her eye as the road began its winding descent towards the valley, and she was just wondering if there would be much water in the river ahead at this time of year when she was forced to jam her foot on the brake.

Her reactions were quick, but even then she only just avoided ploughing into the back of the car wedged on its side against the unforgiving hedge.

CHAPTER TWO

'DAD-DEEE' wailed a little voice, only audible when Bethan switched off her engine, her little car fitting almost completely into a nearby gateway.

The despairing sound was enough to have her out of the car in a flash, with visions of a small child trapped in the crumpled vehicle, apparently the only one *not* unconscious.

Her emotional longing to comfort the terrified child made her want to rush to the car, but sheer common sense and years of training made her pause just long enough to grab her bag and fumble for her mobile phone.

It was the work of seconds to alert the emergency services to the situation and, while she worried that her directions were sketchy, the admirably calm person on the other end of the line seemed to know exactly where they were.

She'd dumped her bag back on her seat and was within a couple of paces of the overturned car when she saw the trickle of escaping moisture running along the road and smelled the unmistakable odour of petrol.

For less than a heartbeat her feet refused to move. The only thing she could think of was her worst memory from her years of training—the badly burned patient who'd been brought into the A and E department late one night during her first week on duty.

The poor man had only tried to be a good Samaritan when he'd witnessed a car crash. He'd been struggling to try to lift the driver out of the wreck, not knowing that the man was already dead, when the car caught fire.

She shook her head to banish the grisly spectre and held her breath against the pervasive odour as she crouched down to peer in through the windscreen.

At first it was difficult to see what had happened inside the vehicle. The impact had flung the occupants' belongings about, and the fact that the whole thing was tipped over onto the driver's side was making the unused seat belts dangle strangely in mid-air.

The sight of fitful movement drew her attention inside the gloom to the child's safety seat in the back, the diminutive child hiccuping as if she'd been sobbing for some time.

'D-Daddy, talk to m-me. Are you all r-right? Please...don't be d-dead...'

Bethan couldn't help her gasp of dismay and hurried round to the roof of the car, rising vertically from the middle of the road.

She stretched across and found that her hand just reached the passenger doorhandle, but when she tried to open it she found it was locked.

'Sweetheart? Can you hear me?' she called, tapping on the window to attract the child's attention, and was delighted when the keening shuddered to a halt.

'Who...who is it?' quavered the little voice. 'Where are y-you?'

'I'm outside the car,' Bethan said stretching up on tiptoe to lean over as far as she could. 'Can you see me now?'

A little head of dark curls turned towards her and she met a pair of familiar dark blue eyes.

'Sam,' she breathed in horror, recognition coming instantly. 'Are you hurt, sweetheart?'

'N-no, but my d-daddy's not t-talking.'

'Well, we'd better see if there's anything we can do to help him,' Bethan said, keeping her tone brisk and friendly in spite of the puddle of fuel spreading rapidly around her feet. 'Can you undo your safety harness?'

'Y-yes, but Daddy said I m-mustn't until he tells me to,' the youngster said hesitantly.

'Well, if he tries to tell you off this time, you can say it was my fault. OK?' Bethan bargained. 'Don't forget to hang on so you don't fall when it comes undone.'

'O-OK,' the child returned, its tone slightly less dubious, and Bethan saw chubby fingers attacking the mechanism. Within seconds there was a click.

'Oops! N-nearly!' came the little voice, accompanying a scuffling sound. 'I n-nearly felled on the floor.'

'Can you climb up on the seat and unlock the door?' Bethan directed. 'Then I can get you and your daddy out.'

She watched the youngster clamber awkwardly over the tilted seat, and crossed her fingers that the expensive vehicle wouldn't have some sort of central locking device to overcome.

Everything in her wanted desperately to urge the child to hurry before disaster struck, but there was nothing she could do to make the precarious climb happen any faster.

Frustrated by the passing of precious time, she peered in at the second silent passenger, wondering just how badly injured he was.

He was slumped heavily against his seat belt, his limbs sprawled at uncomfortable angles and his head lolling against the window between him and the road. How the pane hadn't broken with the impact she didn't know, nor how long he'd been unconscious before she'd arrived on the scene.

'I did it!' said a triumphant voice.

'Good boy, Sam,' she praised as she released the catch and struggled to lift the door.

'I'm not a *boy*!' said a horrified voice, as a curly head emerged around the edge of the door, blue eyes shooting out sparks of indignation. 'I'm a *girl*. I'm Sam-*antha*, and I'm five...n-nearly.'

'Well, I'm very sorry, Sam-*antha*,' Bethan said with a grin widened by sheer relief. 'Now, let's get you out of there.'

She helped the youngster to scramble out onto the side of the car then lifted her into her arms, before turning and hurrying up the road.

'Stop,' Sam shrieked, and tried to wriggle out of her arms. 'What about my d-daddy? He's still s-stuck.'

'Hush, sweetheart. It's all right,' Bethan soothed, as she forced her feet to keep moving in spite of her struggling burden. 'I'm going to get him out as soon as I can, but I need to make sure you're safe first.'

She stopped a little way up the road and lifted the child up onto the top of the solid stone hedge. She'd carefully chosen the position so that if the unthinkable happened and the car exploded Sam would at least be sheltered from most of the blast by the bulk of the nearby beech tree.

'Listen, Sam. This is very important,' Bethan said, catching both grubby paws in her hands and gazing straight into her eyes for emphasis. 'I want you to sit very still up here and wait for me to bring your daddy to you. There could be other cars coming along the road, and I don't want you to get hurt. Do you understand?'

'Y-yes.' The youngster nodded vigorously, her eyes huge and fearful in her little pale face. 'I'm not allowed to go on the road without a g-grown-up.'

'Good girl.' Bethan patted her little denim-clad knee. 'Can you listen out for the sound of sirens and shout as soon as you can hear them? I promise I'll be back as quick as I can.'

She took the brave little girl's smile of agreement with her as she hurried back to the stricken vehicle, her thoughts buzzing around like drunken bumblebees as she tried to work out how she was ever going to get the man out to safety.

It wasn't as if he was small *or* slight—her memory of their first meeting earlier this afternoon told her that he must be at least six feet tall, and his shoulders were broad enough for a swimmer or a rugby player.

He hadn't looked as if he was carrying any surplus weight, but he was still going to be far too heavy for her to lift on her own—and who knew *how* long it was going to be before the emergency services arrived?

She struggled to open the door again, and when she realised that its own weight prevented her from propping it open she had to improvise.

It only took a few seconds to select a handy-sized rock out of those gouged out of the hedge by the car's bumper and a few more to position it in the hinge to prevent it from closing on her.

She cringed when she heard the grating sound and realised that the paintwork would never be the same, then shrugged fatalistically. What did a few more scrapes and scratches on the car's paintwork matter when a man's life was at stake?

'Doctor?' she called, as she leant over the cavernous opening, balancing on her stomach with her feet off the ground in her attempt to reach him. 'Doctor, can you hear me?'

She could just reach his shoulder with her fingertips but couldn't get hold of him well enough to give him a shake—wouldn't dare shake him in case he'd damaged his neck in the crash.

Unfortunately, the smell of petrol was so strong now that the fumes completely filled the car. Bethan knew that the vapour was even more combustible than the liquid trickling down the road outside, and was torn.

What was best?

Should she wait until the emergency services arrived with their specialised equipment to extricate him as safely as possible, and risk having him burn to death if the petrol ignited? Should she climb into the car with him and start checking him over to speed the work of getting him out when they *did* arrive—and risk her own life if she was trapped inside a burning car?

Her eyes scanned the topsy-turvy interior of the car for some sort of inspiration and she gasped in horror.

'Doctor!'

Suddenly there was new urgency in her tone as she scratched at his shoulder with her nails, the sound seeming incredibly loud in the hush of the interior of the car. She had just seen that the ignition light was still on, the red bulb glaring up at her like a malevolent eye in the gloom.

Her heart began to thump unevenly as she realised that the engine hadn't been switched off. The car was sitting there like a primed bomb...

'What...?' The sound was half groan, half speech, but it was the sweetest thing she'd heard in ages.

'Doctor, can you hear me? You've been in an accident and turned your car over.'

Bethan found herself resorting to the childish habit of crossing her fingers as she waited to hear something—anything—from the man crumpled inside the wrecked car.

'S-Sam?' he demanded weakly as he tried to turn his head to look back over his shoulder.

'Don't move your head,' Bethan ordered sharply, ignoring the danger to herself if she slid too far when she hitched herself even further over the edge of the car so that she could place her hand against his head and brace it against his head-rest.

'You might have damaged your neck.'

She watched him squeeze his eyes tightly shut and draw in a ragged breath, very conscious of the heat of his forehead in her hand.

'Sam,' he repeated stubbornly.

'I got her out,' Bethan hastened to reassure him, her thumb stroking the soft hair beside his temple almost by accident. 'She's safe—not a mark on her.'

'Thank God,' he murmured, and she felt some of the tension drain out of him. 'She's had enough pain...'

'Listen,' Bethan interrupted urgently. 'There's petrol leaking onto the road from somewhere, and I don't know how long it'll be before the emergency services can get here. Can you reach far enough to switch off the ignition, without moving your neck, or shall I climb in?'

'I...can do it.'

It seemed to take a long time for him to move, the effort apparently taking as much energy as if his arm had been filled with lead as he fumbled for the dangling keys. She gave a brief sigh of relief when she saw the little light go out, then tensed again when she saw him grimace with the apparently unnecessary effort of pulling the keys out of the ignition.

'Take…keys,' he hissed through gritted teeth as he held them up awkwardly towards her. 'Emergency kit…in the boot. Collar…'

'Of course!' Bethan could have kicked herself. She should have guessed that a doctor working in such a rural area was likely to have more than the usual range of equipment on board.

Her hand felt strangely empty when she released her hold on his head to wriggle back out of the car, but the quicker she could fit the cervical collar on him the sooner she could stop worrying about the stability of his neck.

It took just a moment or two for her to be back at the side of the car, and she thanked her lucky stars that she had kept herself fairly fit when she had to go into her balancing routine again over the edge of the roof of the car.

By the time she'd slid the cervical collar into position, without jarring his neck, and had fastened the Velcro straps to secure it, she felt as if so much blood had rushed to her head that it was about to burst.

'Well done,' he muttered through pale lips, obviously having to concentrate on co-ordinating his speech and breathing. 'Practice obviously makes perfect…even on a tricky job like that… But the next bit's impossible…even if you could strap me to a backboard single-handed… You couldn't get me out because my foot's stuck.'

Bethan's heart sank when she peered down into the footwell for the first time and saw the way the front corner of the car had been deformed on impact.

'It looks as if it's thoroughly trapped between the

accelerator and the side of the car,' she said, trying to make sense of what she could see. 'Can't you move it at all?'

'Not an inch,' he confirmed.

'Well, unless your car's equipped with an industrial-size tin-opener, it looks as if I've got as far as I can without some heavy-duty assistance.'

'They're coming,' called a piping voice from further up the lane, and Bethan raised her head to listen.

'Good girl, Sam. I can hear them, too,' she called back, the familiar sound of sirens in the distance lifting her heart like nothing else could have at that moment. 'Stay nice and still up there, sweetheart, and count how many are coming.'

She looked back down at the trapped man and suddenly realised how grey he was looking.

'I'm sorry,' she apologised quickly. 'I've been so worried about all this petrol everywhere that I didn't think about getting you something for the pain.'

'No...nothing,' he murmured, and groaned when he made the mistake of trying to shake his head.

'Don't be an idiot,' Bethan retorted fiercely over the hissing sound of his indrawn breath. 'When they get here they're going to have to get you out as fast as they can, and I need to get something into you *now* or it won't be effective enough to stop you shouting. Do you *want* to terrify Sam?'

'Of course not,' he denied, obviously stung by the very idea. 'I wouldn't put her through that again...' He stopped abruptly, as though he'd suddenly realised that he'd said more than he'd intended. 'See what I've got in there that'll do the job quickly...without knocking me out completely.'

'Well, you can't have any of the opiates because of the possibility of head injury,' Bethan called up as she crouched in the road beside the car and sorted through the contents of his bag, having climbed down once more. 'And until the ambulance gets here, you haven't got any Entonox. It looks as if this codeine phosphate is going to be the most efficient. At least it doesn't carry the danger of masking any neurological signs.'

He grunted his agreement and managed to co-operate with her while she administered the correct dosage, while hanging upside down.

All the while the banshee wail was drawing closer, gradually separating out into the sounds of several vehicles.

The police car was the first to arrive, closely followed by an ambulance, and Bethan breathed a sigh of relief when she saw the sign showing that there was a paramedic on board.

'Back in a minute,' Bethan said quickly, blessing the fact that the sandals she'd worn today were eminently comfortable as she ran uphill towards the flashing lights.

'You need to keep your vehicles well away,' she warned quickly as she flagged down the police car and bent to speak through the open window. 'The car's leaking petrol and it's spreading across the road.'

'That's *all* we need,' swore the policeman, with a muttered profanity as his eyes swept the scene with practised thoroughness. 'How many trapped? The message didn't say.'

'Just one, now that I've got his daughter out,' Bethan told him, with a brief gesture towards Sam perched in relative safety on the hedge nearby. 'I think he's a local doctor.'

'Not Doc Kent?' demanded the policeman in the

passenger side as he climbed out of the vehicle and signalled to his companion to reverse up the road into the wide gateway behind Bethan's car. 'It looks like his car—although it's a little difficult to recognise it at this angle.'

'We didn't bother with formal introductions,' Bethan said wryly, 'but his daughter's called Sam.'

'That's the one. Josh Kent. A damn good bloke to have on your team.'

Bethan allowed herself a brief memory of the way the good doctor had pitched in to help with the wounded earlier that afternoon and couldn't help but agree. The fact that she was reacting to him so strongly as a man had nothing to do with it...

'How long before the fire crew arrives?' she prompted, dragging herself forcibly back to the fraught situation facing the poor man. 'They're going to have to put something down to prevent that lot igniting before they can cut him out. One accidental spark would set the whole lot off.'

'There's more sirens coming!' called a little voice right on cue. Her announcement coincided with the arrival of the ambulance crew on foot, each of them carrying their emergency bags.

'Hey! That's my princess!' called one of them, a burly man with close-cropped greying hair. 'What are you doing perched right up there? Pretending to be a bird?'

Bethan smiled when she saw him deposit his bag on top of the hedge in favour of whirling the giggling youngster around in what was obviously a well-worn ritual.

Bethan glanced back towards the stricken car and felt a tug on her heartstrings. The poor man could probably hear his daughter's voice as he lay trapped inside, all alone and waiting for someone to come and tell him what was happening.

Bethan took one step in his direction, then made herself pause just long enough to greet the paramedic and put him in the picture.

'His pulse rate's OK and there's no problem with his breathing that I could tell, even though he's partially suspended by his seat belt. He's got a goose egg on his head but his pupils are even and react normally.'

She winced when she remembered how far she'd had to hang into the car to get *those* results—her ribs were going to be complaining tomorrow.

'I've put a collar on him,' she continued briskly, wanting to get back to him. 'And I've given him an injection of codeine, but I'd like to see an IV line up and running into him in case it takes a long time to get him free. When it's time to move him you're going to have a dickens of a job immobilising him on a backboard and he'll probably need some Entonox, although I expect he'll argue the toss over that...'

'Peter Pemberthy,' said the grizzled man, freeing one hand from holding Sam just long enough to shake hands with Bethan. 'You seem to have got everything under control. Almost seems a waste of time, calling us out for this one. Are you one of us?' He tapped the paramedic insignia on his protective uniform.

'Doctor,' Bethan said succinctly, with a fleeting glance over her shoulder towards the trapped man. 'A and E, upcountry. Look, if you don't mind me muscling in I could get that IV line in while you get your kit out and look after Sam.'

'Whatever,' he agreed easily, then smiled down at the youngster in his arms, her face far too serious as she listened to their conversation about her father. 'I never mind having a cuddle instead of working, do I, Princess?' he teased, and tickled her until she giggled again.

As soon as she'd collected the necessary items from the bag Bethan hurried back down the slope to the car.

'Doctor...' she called softly as she leaned into the car again.

He looked very grey and when she saw that his eyes were closed she was worried that he'd lapsed into unconsciousness again.

'Hey, Josh,' she called as she stroked her fingertips down his cheek and felt the rasp of his emerging beard. It felt strange to use his first name when they'd never been introduced, but she hoped the intimacy would help to rouse him.

He stirred and groaned, then opened his eyes to look up at her, his eyes almost painfully blue against the pallor of his skin.

'What's going on...out there?' he demanded. 'How much longer?'

'The police have arrived and are sorting everyone out because of the petrol spilled on the road. I expect they'll be closing the road off completely until we've got you out. The ambulance is standing by with a backboard for when you're ready to be moved. All we're waiting for is the fire crew to get here to douse the area with whatever retardant they use to make the petrol safe, before they start cutting you out.'

For just a second a weary smile creased the corners of his eyes and curved his lips before he struggled to speak.

'We were going to have a barbeque this evening...when we got home...but I had no intention of providing the main course myself.'

Bethan was startled into a chuckle.

'Typical grisly medical sense of humour,' she chided. 'Now, let me have your arm and I'll get this IV up and running so we don't have to use you for target practice in the middle of an exciting bit.'

He grimaced but, to her surprise, didn't argue about the necessity. That made Bethan wonder exactly how much pain he was in—or had he realised that this might end up being a long slow job?

'You're good at that,' he commented quietly when the IV was set up without a hitch. 'Did I hear you trained with Jane?'

'Not *with*, exactly,' Bethan corrected, 'but it was at the same hospital.'

'Not much of a holiday so far,' he murmured. 'You've been in the wrong place at the wrong time twice today.'

'Or in the right place,' she countered. 'It depends on your point of view.'

He smiled wanly and closed his eyes, and Bethan's heart clenched in sympathy when she suddenly realised that it wasn't just the effects of his injuries which were giving him such a drawn appearance. Now that the pain-killing drug was forcing him to relax, she could see that the man looked absolutely exhausted.

'Excuse me, miss?' called a voice, and Bethan looked back up the road to see a fireman wearing protective clothing beckoning to her.

'It looks as if they want me to get out of the way so they can start work,' she said as she started to straighten away from the car.

'Please… Wait!' he called, with what sounded like a touch of panic in his deep voice, and Bethan paused, looking down into his eyes. 'Please… Will you stay…? With Sam?'

For just a second Bethan had thought he was asking her to stay with him and her heart had performed a silly loop inside her—very silly when she considered that she'd only known the man for a matter of hours.

'But I'm a stranger to her,' Bethan objected in surprise when she'd got over her irrational disappointment. 'Wouldn't she feel happier with someone she knows? Won't someone have contacted your wife to tell her what's happened?'

'My wife is...no longer around to take care of Sam,' he said, his voice showing signs of strain. Whether that was due to the topic of conversation or to his physical situation she couldn't tell, but that wasn't important for the moment.

'If you'd rather...get on your way that's all right,' he muttered wearily. 'I'm sure one of the ambulancemen—'

'No,' she interrupted quickly. 'I'll stay with her. I've nowhere important to go and my time's my own.'

For one insane moment she wanted to reach into the car and touch him again—wished she had the right to deliberately offer him the wordless consolation that she really cared what happened to him...

But the fire crew was waiting for her to get out of the way so that they could douse the petrol-coated road, and all she could do was walk away and leave him in his lonely isolation.

'Is my daddy going to be all right?' asked Sam in a very subdued voice. 'Couldn't you lift him out of the car?'

'No, sweetheart. He's much too heavy for me to lift by myself so I decided to let the men with the big muscles do it,' Bethan said, smiling reassuringly down at the youngster, sitting beside her on top of the hedge. 'Anyway, his foot is stuck underneath one of the pedals.'

'Couldn't you get it unstuck?' Sam queried.

'No. My arms weren't long enough to reach so the firemen are going to have to get him unstuck with their special equipment.'

'How?'

Bethan couldn't help the grin that crept over her face. Even though she wasn't yet a mother herself, she'd come across enough children in her work to know that 'how' and 'why' were perhaps the most frequently used words.

Big blue eyes were looking up at her, filled with open curiosity, and she settled herself down to explain exactly how the rescue services would release the little girl's father.

'You mean they're going to chop his car up?' she exclaimed in horror when Bethan told her what the enormous metal jaws were for. 'He's going to be awful cross.'

'I don't suppose he'll be too cross if the firemen manage to get his foot free so he can climb out,' Bethan said comfortingly.

Sam was quiet for a moment, and Bethan noticed that when the big hydraulic machine took its first high-powered bite into the structure of the once-gleaming car her eyes grew enormous and she lost what little colour she'd regained.

'It's all my fault,' she whispered, so softly that Bethan almost didn't hear her.

'What's your fault, sweetheart?' she questioned gently, curving one arm around her little shoulders.

'The crash,' she said, her eyes filling up with tears as she watched the crew dismantling the car around her father. 'I didn't mean it,' she said, as the first silvery drop overflowed and ran down to outline the curve of her cheek. 'I didn't *mean* to 'stract him when he was driving.'

The last words emerged as a despairing wail and she turned towards Bethan and buried her face against her shoulder, her little body racked by sobs.

For the next half-hour Bethan's attention was torn between watching the emergency services struggle to extricate the trapped man from his car and trying to console his little child who believed utterly that it was all her fault that he was there in the first place.

Finally, once the roof had been removed, the ambulancemen were able to take the precaution of sliding a lightweight backboard between Josh's body and the seat. Then they dared to move the car just enough so that they could free his foot.

Bethan waited until he'd been loaded onto a stretcher before she climbed down from her perch on the wall and held her arms out for Sam.

'Let's go and see if you can give your daddy a kiss before they take him for his ride,' Bethan suggested, careful to pitch her voice loudly enough that the ambulance crew knew that they were coming over.

Sure enough, by the time they reached the back of the ambulance one corner of the blanket had been strategically positioned to cover the IV from Sam's sight.

'He's all wrapped up like my teddy-bear when I put him to bed,' the little girl said in a stage whisper.

'I heard that,' said a gruff voice as Josh pulled the Entonox mask down with his free hand, the words followed by a growl.

Sam gave a watery giggle.

'That's the noise my daddy makes when he's going to chase me into bed,' she told Bethan.

'Well, this time, it's *Daddy* who's in bed,' Bethan pointed out. 'Does he usually give you a kiss good-night?'

'Yes.' She nodded, her expression showing that she couldn't quite decide whether she ought to be fascinated or frightened by the unexpected switch in roles.

'I'm waiting for my kiss,' prompted a deep voice, and Bethan stepped forward so that Sam could lean down to press her lips very gently on her father's forehead.

'I'm sorry, Daddy,' she whispered, resting one grubby hand very gingerly against his cheek. 'I didn't mean to 'stract you and make you crash the car. Don't be cross.'

'Oh, Sam, I'm not cross with you,' he said huskily. 'It wasn't your fault.'

'Really?'

'Really,' he repeated as firmly as the collar would allow. 'Now, I need another kiss.'

'It's your turn,' Sam announced, straightening up suddenly, her little arm tightening around Bethan's neck to push her towards the mummified figure... Except that there was nothing remotely mummified about the startled expression on his face when he registered what his daughter had said—or Bethan's reaction to it.

'Sam...' he began, but his husky words were overwhelmed by Peter Pemberthy's sly contribution.

'That sounds like a good idea,' he said heartily with a wicked twinkle in his eyes. 'A quick kiss from a pretty lady to send him on his way, then we must get moving.'

Bethan gazed down at him, wondering how a man in such a defenceless position could seem so full of latent power. She made the mistake of looking into his eyes and was trapped in their deep blue depths.

'One for luck?' he murmured softly, the slightly throaty sound of his baritone voice raising prickles of awareness all over her body.

One dark eyebrow was raised in blatant challenge, and for the first time in her life she totally ignored all her grandmother's teachings about ladylike restraint and, throwing caution to the wind, bent towards him.

CHAPTER THREE

Two hours later Bethan's lips still seemed to be tingling from that kiss, in spite of the fact that she'd tried to keep her mind too occupied to think about it.

The back doors of the ambulance had already been shut and the motor running by the time she'd realised that she had no idea where Sam lived or whether there would be anyone at home to look after her.

Although it hadn't been the most satisfactory arrangement, she'd secured the little child into the back seat of her own car with an adult-sized seat belt and had set off after the ambulance.

By the time she'd managed to park her car at the hospital and had carried a terrified Sam all the way to the emergency waiting room Joshua Kent had been nowhere in sight.

The little girl had clung to Bethan, refusing to be put down. It had almost been as if she'd been afraid of being abandoned, and it had taken some time to calm Sam down with reassurances that the other doctors were looking after her daddy.

Bethan's own thoughts were less positive, with the spectre of spinal cord injury hovering menacingly in her mind.

She made certain that someone would come and tell her as soon as there was any news. She elicited the information that he'd already been sent up for X-rays of his spine and a brain scan, but all she could do was settle down for the interminable wait, trying to find ways to take Sam's mind off what might be happening to her father.

Finally, the long, event-filled day caught up with the little girl and she fell asleep in Bethan's arms.

That was when the memory of *that kiss* returned to plague Bethan and flood her cheeks with fire.

She'd only intended to brush his forehead fleetingly, the way Sam had, but at the last moment an unexpected streak of devilment had risen up in answer to the dark challenge in his eyes and she'd chosen instead to press her lips directly over his.

She shivered as she remembered how warm they'd felt against her own and how softly pliant as he'd caressed hers with them, finally parting them to flick just the tip of a wickedly sexy tongue along the curve of them.

She'd straightened up as swiftly as if she'd been stung, hoping her startled gasp hadn't travelled to the interested onlookers.

He had heard it, though, and despite his physical predicament it was obvious just from the expression in his eyes that he had been all too aware that she'd been unable to stop herself responding to him.

She shifted slightly on the uncomfortably meagre upholstery of one of the waiting-room seats, grateful that at least there were enough of them for some of Sam's weight to be supported by something other than her inexperienced lap.

A quick glance up at the clock told her that it would soon be ten o'clock, and until she was able to go up to whichever ward Sam's father had been admitted to she had no way of asking him what to do with his daughter for the rest of the night.

Luckily she'd remembered earlier to find a phone to warn her hotel that she would probably be rather late, but for the moment she was stuck with a sleeping child, a collection of empty soft drink cans and sandwich wrappers and half a polystyrene cup of stone-cold coffee.

There was the sound of some sort of argument going on somewhere further along the corridor, gradually getting closer.

For a moment Bethan was worried that the noise would wake Sam, but the child hardly stirred—even when the door to the waiting room was unceremoniously pushed open.

Bethan's eyes widened when she saw the tableau in the doorway.

There were four people in all—a trio of hospital personnel, wearing variations on a theme of the same disapproving expression, and Dr Joshua Kent.

Except this was Josh Kent as she had never expected to see him, with his dark hair standing out endearingly at all angles around his beard-shadowed face as he tried to keep his exhausted body upright on a borrowed pair of crutches.

With the memory of their kiss so clear in her mind she hadn't known what her reaction was going to be when she saw him again, but she certainly hadn't expected this surge of awareness.

From where she was sitting Bethan could see that his dark blue jeans had been split right up the seam of his injured leg. There were safety pins holding the edges together and, through the interesting gaps between them, she could catch glimpses of what looked like a heavy bandage or even a cast, reaching above his knee.

She completed her inventory of his visible injuries with a wince for the goose egg he was sporting high up on one side of his forehead, and was just in time to see his fierce expression soften when he saw the way his daughter was sprawled across Bethan's lap.

'Are you ready to take Sam and me home?' he asked with a beguiling smile. His voice still bore a hint of the intriguing huskiness which had helped to spur her into her unaccustomed boldness in kissing him, and every protective instinct inside her sprang to the alert.

'I didn't realise that you'd be kept hanging around for so many hours,' he continued, dragging her attention back from their wandering in forbidden territory. 'If I'd known, I'd have sent you on ahead and got a taxi for myself.'

'Dr Kent, I must protest,' the young white-coated doctor behind him in the doorway interrupted before Bethan had a chance to reply to the barefaced cheek of the man. What presumption! As if she was a close friend who had nothing better to do than wait around with his child until he was ready for transportation elsewhere!

'Shh!' he hissed quickly, obviously intent on silencing the younger man. 'Don't wake my daughter up.'

'Sorry,' he said at a much lower volume. 'But you shouldn't be leaving the hospital tonight. The X-rays didn't show any evidence of injury to your spine and the scan seems clear, but you've had a blow to the head and you were unconscious for some time. You should be kept in under observation overnight.'

'Ah, but I *will* be under supervision,' he retorted with the panache of a conjurer pulling a rabbit out of a hat. 'My chauffeur is perfectly well qualified to special me for the rest of the night, aren't you, sweetheart?'

The outrageous words were accompanied by an incongruously pleading look, which stilled the sharp retort that hovered on Bethan's tongue.

For an endless second she gazed at him across the small room and tried to work out what was going on.

It was no surprise that he knew she had medical training—he'd seen her in action this afternoon—but why on earth was he implying an intimacy between them that didn't exist...in spite of that kiss?

It was when she saw his eyes flicker from her to the sleeping child in her arms that things became clearer.

He must have known how upset Sam had been and didn't want to put her through the additional trauma of finding her father confined to a hospital bed.

'Well, I don't think *your* car's going to be going anywhere very fast,' she said obliquely, and was rewarded by a grateful grin that had her pulse playing hopscotch.

'You *have* had experience of taking care of people after head injuries?' the young doctor queried warily, directing his words towards Bethan, as if he had conceded that his patient wasn't going to listen to him. 'You know what to look for?'

'If not, the hospital where I trained weren't doing their job properly,' Bethan pointed out sweetly and, when he still looked dubious, decided on the spur of the moment that a little boasting might be in order. 'I've been on A and E for the last six months, but I've also done my time in Surgery, Paediatrics and Geriatrics, not to mention Obs and Gynae.'

'As I told you,' Josh Kent butted in smugly, 'she's eminently qualified to keep an eye on a minor bump on the head.'

The small knot of staff were muttering among

themselves as they gave in to the inevitable and went back to their more tractable patients.

'Quick,' he muttered as he shuffled warily on his one sound foot, obviously trying to sort out how to turn round without having the crutches slide apart and deposit him on the floor. 'Let's get out of here before they change their minds.'

'How?' Bethan asked, not wanting to wake the sleeping child to make her walk out to the car.

'How what?'

'*How* do we get out of here?' she elaborated patiently. '*You* certainly aren't in a fit state to carry Sam, and my arms are nearly dropping off after holding her for so long. I know I wouldn't be able to carry her all the way back to the car.'

'Damn,' he muttered, and slumped one shoulder against the doorframe, his face suddenly becoming more drawn than ever.

Bethan's heart went out to him. She could see that he'd reached the end of his tether long ago, and his exhaustion meant that he was barely hanging on.

'Can you manage to perch yourself on a seat long enough to hold Sam while I find a wheelchair?' she suggested. 'Then you could wait with her by the entrance while I bring the car round.'

He scowled darkly and she could see that the idea of being reliant on someone pushing him around in a wheelchair didn't sit well with his pride. Then he looked down at Sam's innocent oblivion and she could almost hear him swallow the bitter pill.

'OK,' he muttered on a tired sigh, and positioned the crutches again to move towards her. 'Anything to get out of this place.'

It was another quarter-hour before Bethan had finally settled her passengers into her car.

The passenger seat had needed to be pushed back to its full extent to accommodate Josh's immobile knee, and she'd had to be very creative with the seat belts on the back seat to hold the soundly sleeping child safely for the journey.

'Right, sir,' she said crisply as she clicked her own belt into position and turned towards him expectantly. 'Where are we going?'

Several seconds passed in silence before he spoke.

'For a moment I'd forgotten that you're a stranger to the area,' he said with a trace of surprise in his voice. 'We need to go all the way back the way we came—almost into Pendruccombe. The crash actually happened less than a mile from the house.'

'Is it as pretty as it sounds?' she asked, taking the conversation away from the topic of his accident as she put the car in motion. 'I was exploring after I left the show and saw the name on a road sign. It sounded intriguing so I wanted to find out what it looked like.'

'Just a typical Cornish village, I suppose,' he said dismissively. 'A small collection of cottages and houses grouped around the church and the village green, and surrounded by farms and moorland—one of hundreds in the county—nothing special.'

'So it's just all the unusual musical names that make them seem a bit…magical?' she asked wistfully.

'There's nothing very magical about them in the grip of a winter blizzard when the wind's whipping the snow off the tors and dumping it in ten-foot snow-drifts on top of us,' he said grimly. 'Then the fact of living in an isolated rural community can be a death sentence if you're taken ill.'

'I can imagine,' Bethan said with a shiver. 'Unable to get out for help, and help unable to get to you…

But, surely, this time of year must be compensation for that?'

'Thousands of extra inhabitants, flooding into the county on holiday each summer, bring their own problems, believe me.'

'Isn't that a good thing? Surely the income from tourism is essential to Cornwall's economy?'

'It also means that a frighteningly large proportion of the residents have to rely on seasonal work to support their families, and in a poor season—when the weather's less than perfect—it can mean disaster.'

'But—'

'Then there's the strain the visitors put on the fragile environment and the limited water supply, not to mention clogging up the roads in caravans and frying themselves to a crisp on the beaches.'

Bethan couldn't help chuckling. 'I hope the Tourist Board realise not to ask you to promote their industry,' she joked. 'You sound as if you'd rather Cornwall's attractions were a well-kept secret, only to be appreciated by residents.'

'Well,' Josh grumbled and she thought she could detect a hint of sheepishness in his tone, 'I used to come here when I was a kid and it seemed like such a peaceful place then...an absolute haven after city life.'

'Is that why you moved back here?' she queried as she slowed to take the turning down the lane towards Pendruccombe. She was only half concentrating on the conversation while she silently marvelled at how much faster the journey had been with him in the car, even though it was now fully dark and there was no scenery to look at to pass the time.

Following the ambulance on the way to the hospital, time had seemed to drag by interminably while she'd worried about his injuries.

Now she knew that, apart from a badly twisted foot and a possible torn ligament in his knee, he'd suffered little more than bumps and bruises which, considering the state of the car and what *could* have happened, was pretty miraculous.

She'd almost forgotten her question when he finally answered.

'I suppose it was partly nostalgia that brought me back,' he said into the dark confines of her little car, and she heard a strange undertone in his voice. 'I wanted the same carefree atmosphere to surround Sam so that she could feel safe…'

'Safe?' Bethan repeated when his voice died away and left her wondering what had made him choose that particular word.

'Anything's got to be better than the rough end of Birmingham,' he quipped, but the humour sounded forced.

Bethan didn't pursue the matter. Her headlights had just picked out the warning sign for the ford and she'd realised where they were.

'It was just down here that it happened, wasn't it?' She slowed as she reached the slight bend before the road swooped towards the river at the bottom of the hill, worried that the road might still be partially obstructed by the remains of his car.

'Oh, it's all gone,' she said in surprise when all she could see was a series of vicious gouges in the Cornish hedge and a large stain on the road to show where the accident had happened.

'The emergency services are pretty quick about clearing things like that away,' Josh said as she put the car in motion again. 'The roads are too narrow to leave it there for long before someone else would plough into it and they'd have another wreck to sort out.'

They reached the ford, and Bethan wasn't sure whether she was disappointed that there was only an unremarkable trickle of water to cross or relieved not to have to face anything more challenging, especially after everything else that had filled the day.

They passed through a small wooded area and then Bethan caught sight of the first evidence that they had reached Pendruccombe—a cottage, with light streaming out of a window to make a golden pathway onto the edge of the road.

'Take the turning opposite that cottage,' he directed. 'The light almost acts as a signpost towards the house. It's just a short driveway, leading to a paved yard, and there should be a light over the door to show you where to park.'

Bethan followed his directions but there didn't seem to be any light on.

'Blast it,' he muttered as she drew up beside the door. 'Don't tell me she's not in.'

'Who?' Bethan queried, startled by the sudden clenching around her heart at the thought that he'd been expecting a woman to be waiting for him.

'Molly Wonnacott,' he said distractedly. 'My housekeeper.'

'Perhaps you're so late that she's gone home,' Bethan suggested reasonably as she released her seat belt and opened the car door, her thoughts already turning towards the likelihood that Sam would sleep through yet another transfer.

'Hardly,' he said testily. 'This *is* her home.'

Bethan froze with one foot on the ground and the other still in the car.

'There *will* be someone in the house tonight to keep an eye on you, won't there?' she questioned urgently, her mind filled with a picture of him lapsing into unconsciousness with only his frightened daughter around.

'There *should* be,' he said, the words ending on a groan when he tried to swivel round in his seat to open his own door.

'Let me do that,' Bethan ordered sharply. 'You're in no fit state to try any contortions.'

She paused just long enough to watch him subside in frustration, then hurried round to his side and pulled the door fully open, before crouching down to ease his feet out onto the ground.

'Here you are,' she said as she retrieved his crutches from the space behind his seat then propped them in the angle of the door. 'Give me your arms and I'll help you slide forward to the edge of the seat. Then you can get your weight in the right place to balance.'

She heard him catch his breath twice as they completed the manoeuvre, but he must have been gritting his teeth because he didn't utter a sound.

She shadowed him like a worried sheepdog as he made his halting way up to the door, then had to grab his elbow when he tried to reach into his pocket for his keys and nearly overbalanced.

'You'll have to get them,' Josh said, resting his forehead against the door in defeat. 'Otherwise I might just as well go to sleep where I fall because I'd never get up again.'

Just the thought of putting her hand into the pocket of his jeans to fish for his keys was enough to bring Bethan out in a sweat. He might be injured and exhausted but that didn't seem to mean anything to her body's appreciation of his masculinity, and the thought of doing something so intimate…

Wordlessly she stepped up behind him and slid her arm around his waist, praying that she would be able to find the opening without having to fumble around too much.

She'd noticed earlier on today that the jeans were worn enough to look comfortable, and now she knew how well they fitted his body, her fingers tunnelling down the slight hollow between the ridge of his hip-bone and the flat plane of his belly.

'Got them,' she announced, all too conscious that her voice sounded quite breathless as she dragged the worn leather case from its warm, dark resting-place, dragging the lining of his pocket out with the keys in her haste.

'It's the big old-fashioned one,' he said, the husky tone back in his deep voice again. 'It sometimes sticks a bit so you might have to jiggle it.'

The door unlocked on the first try but the hinges gave a 'house of horror' creak when she swung it open to reveal an apparently cavernous dark hallway. Bethan had to swallow, suddenly strangely nervous about going into the old house.

'I'll switch on the lights while you get Sam,' his deep voice said right behind her, and she jumped sky-high and whirled to face him as he loomed over her.

She drew in a steadying breath.

'R-right,' she stammered, her heart pounding at the base of her throat, and she scuttled back to the car.

'Where do you want her?' she whispered when she carried a miraculously sleeping Sam into the house a few minutes later. She'd followed the trail of lights and found him leaning against a heavy kitchen table with a sheet of paper in his hand.

'Damn,' he said quietly but forcefully. 'Damn, damn, damn.'

'That good?' she asked, keeping her voice down in deference to the sleeping child, but she couldn't help a reminiscent smile creeping over her face. 'For a moment you sounded almost like my grandmother.'

'Your grandmother?' he murmured in disbelief, a look of amazement on his face. 'How?'

'She was a very upright, churchgoing lady who didn't approve of people swearing all the time, but if something *really* went wrong she used to say, "Damn, damn, double damn, two blasts, a hellfire and a bugger you," all in one breath.'

Bethan's mimicry of her grandmother's exasperated delivery of the profane litany was enough to startle him into a hushed laugh and for the first time in hours he looked like the charismatic man she'd first seen at the show.

'And just what sort of calamity would bring that on?' he demanded softly, his attention caught in spite of his exhaustion.

'Oh, things like…the day she'd just finished pegging out a long row of white sheets and towels on the washing line and it broke and dumped the lot in the dirt.'

'Oh, no.' Josh winced at the mental image, but his deep blue eyes were gleaming with life again.

In spite of the fact that it was getting late and her arms were aching with the weight of the sleeping child, something about this man called out to her the way no other ever had, and she found herself wanting to prolong the conversation.

'Or the day she left the garden gate open and the neighbour's puppy came in and dug up all the plants she'd just bedded out.'

'I can see that both of those would warrant the whole litany,' he agreed, before glancing down at the paper in his hand and falling silent again.

'How much of a litany does your note warrant?' she asked, shifting Sam against her other shoulder.

'It's from Molly, telling me that her sister's been taken ill. She's gone to find out how serious it is and hopes to be back tomorrow.'

'And…?'

Bethan had a feeling as if she were waiting for the other shoe to drop.

'And…before you go back to your hotel and try to persuade them to give you something to eat, I'm going to have to ask you to stay here a bit longer because I'm going to need your help to get Sam to bed.'

Bethan was silent for a moment while she quickly sorted through the ramifications of the new situation.

Yes, he was going to need her help with Sam, but he was going to need a great deal more than that, including regular observations over the next few hours to check on his reactions after the head injury.

Still, there would be plenty of time after Sam was settled to thrash out the rest of his needs, whether he wanted to or not.

'OK,' she agreed simply. 'Tell me where to take her.'

He tried to insist on leading the way so that he could turn on the bathroom light to shine into Sam's bedroom, but it was impossible. It was going to take him some time to learn the technique for going upstairs on crutches, and her arms wouldn't wait that long.

While Bethan laid Sam on the bed and took her outer clothing off she could hear him muttering under his breath while he struggled. By the time she had the child settled under the covers he'd hobbled into the bathroom to fetch a warm flannel so that Bethan could wash his daughter's little tearstained face.

He gestured silently towards a rather disreputable-looking lamb, lying on the pillow, and Bethan placed it in the child's grasp.

'Daddy?' she murmured, amazing Bethan that she'd slept through everything else going on, but would surface once she was in her own bed with her favourite toy.

'I'm here, Sam,' he said gently. 'Go to sleep and I'll see you in the morning.'

She was asleep again almost before he'd finished speaking, a little smile on her face as she wrapped one arm tightly around the much-loved animal.

'Leave the door ajar so I can hear her if she calls in the night,' he whispered as they left the room.

'Which one is your room?' she questioned as he made his laborious way along the landing.

'I'm here, right next door.' He nodded towards the open door beside them. 'Close enough to hear.'

'How many other bedrooms are there up here?' She looked round the shadowy corners and counted two more doors apart from the bathroom.

'Molly's and a spare,' he said with the beginnings of a frown. 'Any reason for the question?'

'I was just wondering which one you'd like me to borrow for the night,' she said, taking the bull by the horns and hoping her tone was cool enough to hide the fact that she had severe misgivings about his reaction.

'Borrow?' he said, the frown pleating accordion-like across his forehead. 'You want to stay here for the night?'

'Well, you should by rights still be in hospital under observation and my hotel is too far away for me to drive backwards and forwards,' she pointed out logically. 'Besides, I'm hoping you're going to let me loose in your kitchen before long. I'll have missed my dinner at the hotel and I'm starving.'

Bethan knew she should be feeling slightly guilty about broadsiding him like this, especially when he looked just about ready to fall asleep where he stood, but she had a feeling that this was the *only* way she would be able to coerce him into agreeing.

He opened his mouth and for a moment it looked as if he was going to argue the point, but then he shrugged.

'I don't suppose for a moment that I'm going to need you in the night, but I can see that you're determined to stay and do your bit. Anyway, I owe you a meal, at least,' he said, and turned to go downstairs again.

'It would make far more sense if you let *me* go down,' Bethan pointed out quietly when she saw the way he paused at the top, his shoulders slumping at the thought of negotiating the whole flight all over again.

'I'm sure I'll be able to find something edible,' she prompted persuasively, 'and it would give you plenty of time in the bathroom to start getting yourself ready for bed. Don't forget, it's going to take you a lot longer than usual.'

'As if I needed reminding,' he muttered disgustedly. 'Are you sure you don't mind fending for yourself?'

'No problem,' she said confidently, pausing just long enough to watch him make his way back along the landing, before she set off down the stairs.

She'd barely noticed the room when she'd been in

here earlier but the kitchen was delightful, the pale wood cupboards gleaming with years of care and use.

The same seemed to be true of the whole house— at least the parts she'd seen so far. The walls were decorated in a range of the paler, more modern colours, but the furniture seemed to be composed almost entirely of treasured family heirlooms.

Heirlooms with a difference, she thought as she looked at the dresser full of china against one wall. These weren't the sort of things that children had to be warned away from for fear that they might damage them, but the sort that wore each scratch and dent as a badge of honour.

The sound of footsteps up above made her realise that she'd been standing idle, in spite of the fact that her stomach had started growling at her hours ago.

'Well, Molly certainly keeps a well-stocked fridge,' she murmured when she opened the door for a look and, bearing in mind the fact that the poor man needed sleep almost more than he needed food, settled on basic bacon and eggs for the sake of speed.

While everything was cooking she contemplated eating her own meal at the kitchen table but when she caught sight of the large wooden tray, propped against the side of the sink unit, she had a better idea.

She made a pot of tea, buttered a plate of crusty home-made bread and found a jar of strawberry jam made not three weeks ago, according to the handwritten label.

She was about to load two piping-hot plates of food onto the tray and was just anticipating the pleasure on his face when she presented it to him when there was a crash directly overhead.

CHAPTER FOUR

THE loaded plates were virtually dropped onto the table before Bethan took off at a run.

All the way up the stairs she had terrible visions of what she would find when she got there.

Had Josh had a problem with his crutches and slipped? Had he suffered delayed concussion and passed out on the floor? Had he hit his head again? Was he unconscious? Bleeding? Had he lapsed into a coma?

'Damn,' she heard when she reached the top of the stairs. 'Damn, damn, damn.'

Bethan almost laughed with relief. At least she had proof that he was conscious.

She reached the bathroom door and went to knock, but the door wasn't closed.

'Are you all right?' she asked as she pushed it open and stuck her head round the edge.

'No, I'm not,' he snarled and glared up at her from the floor.

Bethan had to bite her tongue to stop herself from laughing.

It looked as if he had managed perfectly well to wash his upper half, even going so far as to shave a layer of villainous stubble off his jaw, but when he'd tried to remove his jeans disaster seemed to have struck with a vengeance.

'Don't you dare laugh,' he said through gritted teeth, his eyes shooting sparks at her like a wild animal at bay.

'Or else what?' she heard herself say as she stepped over his fallen crutches to reach him. 'You'd have to catch me to punish me, and at the moment you look as helpless as a whale stranded on a beach.'

'You don't have to rub it in,' he grumbled. 'I know only too well what I must look like.'

Bethan doubted that he would look at himself the way she was. He might be stuck ignominiously on his back, with his jeans tangled out of reach around his ankles, but the body on display at her feet was as well proportioned as any athlete's. The broad shoulders and lean torso were every bit as tanned and muscular as she'd imagined, and even the heavy strapping on one knee couldn't detract from the powerful length of his legs.

She flexed her fingers as she wondered what the dark pattern of hairs on his chest would feel like. Would they be as silky as they looked, or—?

'Are you just going to stand there, gloating?' Josh demanded with a hint of petulance as he looked up at her.

'As if I would,' she countered as she crouched to begin the job of untangling him, firmly forcing her eyes to concentrate on their task rather than continually straying up towards his plain, denim-coloured underwear or back to the fascinating whorls of hair across the width of his chest.

'You could have asked me to help,' she pointed out as she draped the offending jeans over the edge of the bath and bent to retrieve his crutches.

'I thought I could cope,' he grumbled when she held out her hands to help him to regain his feet. 'But when one foot got stuck I forgot which was the injured leg and tried to pitch my whole weight on it.'

'Did you do yourself any more damage?' she asked

when she'd helped him to lower himself to the edge of the bath. 'Did you hit anything on the way down?'

'I wouldn't know—everything's still aching from the last lot.'

Bethan tried to give him a visual once-over, without getting distracted by the mostly naked body in front of her, then gave up. He was a doctor, for heaven's sake. If he'd injured something he'd be able to tell her.

'Have you finished in here?' she asked when the room seemed to grow smaller by the minute, suddenly remembering the meal she'd abandoned so hastily. 'If you're ready to get into bed I'll bring your food up.'

'You don't have to do that,' he objected swiftly as he positioned the crutches and gingerly manoeuvred himself upright. 'I didn't ask you to drive us home so you could be a servant, cooking meals and fetching and carrying.'

'And I'm not offering to be one. There just didn't seem to be much point in cooking for one when it wouldn't take any longer to do it for two.'

'In that case, I accept with alacrity,' he said with a grin that didn't quite manage to hide how bone-weary he was.

'I'd better go down and get it, then. I was just about to put the plates on the tray when it sounded as if you were coming through the ceiling to join me. All I can say is it's a good job you haven't got a dog or your supper would be history by now!'

Bethan knew she was talking too much, but suddenly the thought of sharing a meal with a semi-naked man—even an injured semi-naked man—was scrambling her brain. The only thing she didn't know was whether the idea was making her nervous or whether it was excitement she was feeling...especially as they would be in his bedroom together.

'Pull yourself together,' she muttered, as she checked the tray and discovered that there was no cutlery on it. 'He's hardly in a fit state to ravish you, even if he was interested.'

But if he *wasn't* interested why had he responded so quickly to what should have been a platonic kiss? asked the little voice of logic inside her head.

'Oh, shut up,' she said, then grimaced. 'Talking to myself now. Next stop, a really cosy padded room on the funny farm!'

By the time she'd carried the tray upstairs he'd managed to get himself onto his bed, but was still having a fight with the bedclothes.

'I would never have believed how frustrating it could be to have one knee out of commission,' he exclaimed while she cleared a space on the top of his chest of drawers to deposit her burden. 'I can't imagine what it must be like for people stiffening up through osteoarthritis. At least I know my problem is finite. They know theirs is only going to get worse.'

'It only goes to prove the old saying that you can't really know someone's troubles until you've walked a mile in their shoes,' Bethan quipped as she helped to straighten the covers for him.

'I'll certainly be more understanding of what my older patients are going through,' he agreed. 'Now, stop tormenting me with that delicious smell.'

'Yes, sir!' she said with a mocking salute and turned to get his plate.

They ate together in such a companionable silence that Bethan wondered what she'd been worried about—the attraction she'd imagined she'd felt between them must have been nothing more than wishful thinking.

Far from trying to take advantage of the fact that the two of them were in his bedroom by starting a seduction, he was doing more yawning than anything else by the time she'd poured a second cup of tea.

She was just thinking that she ought to give his reactions a quick check before he fell asleep when there was a cry from the room next door. Instantly he was wide awake again.

'That's Sam,' he muttered as he flung the covers back. 'Can you pass me those wretched crutches? I must go to her.'

'No, you mustn't,' Bethan contradicted with a hand raised, making no attempt to reach for the dreaded props as she put her cup down. '*I'll* go and see what she wants.'

'But you're a stranger,' he objected. 'It would frighten her to find you in her room.'

'Hardly a stranger,' she said with a chuckle. 'We spent several hours together this evening, getting to know each other... And, anyway, you're in no fit state to do anything for her.'

He subsided at the reminder, but he obviously wasn't happy at being thwarted in his wish to go to his child.

'Of course, you're right,' he conceded. 'It's just...she sometimes has nightmares and the accident today might have triggered one.'

'Daddy?' called the little voice again, its tone almost demanding.

'I don't think it's a nightmare this time,' Bethan said. 'It sounds more as if she wants attention, but I promise to help you go to her if she needs you.'

'OK,' he agreed, and with a sigh dropped his head wearily back against the pile of pillows.

'Bethan?' The youngster questioned in surprise when she found the switch for her little bedside light, then a look of panic crossed her face. 'What are *you* doing here? Where's my daddy? Is he all right?'

'He's going to be fine, Sam,' she said reassuringly as she sat beside the child on the edge of her bed and wrapped an arm around her slender shoulders. 'He's in his bed, too, because he's got a bruised knee.'

'Can…can I see him?'

'Of course you can, sweetheart. Then you'll know he's safe.' She wrapped the bedspread around the youngster and scooped her up out of the bed to carry her through to the next room.

'I've got a visitor for you, Dr Kent,' she said, making her tone sound very official, as if he were a patient in a hospital. 'It's someone who wants some reassurance that her daddy's all right.'

'Hello, monster,' Josh said with a smile and open arms. 'Have you come to tuck me into bed and give me a kiss?'

Bethan deposited her burden gently on the bed and, when the little girl immediately flung her arms around his neck, had to turn away under the pretext of stacking their used utensils on the tray when her eyes threatened to fill with sympathetic tears.

It was several minutes before the real reason for Sam's wakefulness surfaced, and Bethan had to chuckle.

'Daddy, I need you to carry me to the bathroom,' Sam said in a stage whisper.

'I'm sorry, did I forget her slippers?' Bethan said with a smile. 'She doesn't need to get chilly feet at this time of night and I don't mind carrying her.'

There was a peculiar silence in the room as they both looked at her as if she'd said something strange.

'I'm sorry, Bethan. When you undressed her... I thought you knew,' he said slowly as he glanced down at his little daughter. 'Sam's still having physiotherapy to get her back on her feet after reconstructive surgery on her leg.'

'But...' She stopped and shook her head, gazing down at the little girl in surprise. 'I've been with her for hours today and never noticed a thing. I thought she was just clinging to me and wanting to be carried because of the accident.'

'It's a long story,' he said, with a meaningful look in his daughter's direction to let Bethan know that he didn't want to go into it with the subject listening.

'She's recently had her last operation, we hope,' he added with an extra hug, 'and now it's just going to take a bit of time to build up her strength before she's running around as good as new—better, in fact, eh, Sam?'

'In that case, may I offer my humble services as a pack pony?' Bethan said with a smile. 'I do a very good line in return trips to the bathroom.'

Sam giggled and held her arms out trustingly to Bethan.

It only took a couple of minutes to help her make herself comfortable, and while they were there Bethan helped Sam to change into a cartoon-covered nightshirt.

Under the bathroom light she could see the livid scars of recent surgery, mute testimony of the pain this little child had endured in her short life, but made no comment.

'Now you can kiss Daddy goodnight and I'll tuck you back into bed,' she said as she picked Sam up and carried her back to her father's room. 'Then you can both get a good night's sleep.'

She propped one knee on the side of Josh's bed and helped Sam to lean forward to give her father a kiss and hug.

'Now it's your turn,' she announced, and looked up at Bethan expectantly.

'Of course, sweetheart,' Bethan said, and a warm glow surrounded her heart at the spontaneous invitation from the sweet little girl. She pressed a kiss to her smooth cheek, breathing in the scent of sunshine and soap from her skin.

'I don't mean *me*!' Sam giggled and squirmed in her arms. 'It's your turn to kiss *Daddy* again.'

Shock made Bethan's eyes whip across to meet his, and once their eyes caught she didn't seem to be able to look away.

As she watched, the deep blue seemed to darken still further and she suddenly realised that she might not be the only one affected by the strange tension between them.

'Ah, Sam…' she began, not quite knowing what to say as the strangely expectant silence stretched between them endlessly.

Embarrassment was causing heat to crawl up her face, but it was more because she was tempted to comply with the little girl's edict that she should kiss her father than because she was averse to the idea.

'It's all right, Sam. I'm not quite ready to go to sleep yet so I can have my kiss later,' her father said huskily, his eyes seeming to gleam with unholy glee as he recognised Bethan's discomfort.

She could put up with that as long as he didn't realise the true reason for it, Bethan thought as she carried the diminutive troublemaker back to her room.

'Will you be here in the morning?' Sam demanded as Bethan pulled the covers up and smoothed them across the little body. 'Daddy won't be able to carry me with his sticks.'

'I'll be here until Mrs Wonnacott gets back from her visit to her sister,' Bethan promised. 'We don't want your daddy bouncing you down the stairs for breakfast, do we?'

Sam giggled again, but this time it had a sleepy edge.

'Sleep tight, sweetheart,' Bethan whispered, and allowed herself to stroke the silky hair just once before she tiptoed out and pulled the door partway closed.

She paused for a moment in the shadowy hallway to savour the brief taste of something special. The situation might have been fraught, but she'd thoroughly enjoyed looking after Sam today. It had been a glimpse into a fascinating world which she might never see again...

'*Enough*,' she breathed crossly and squared her shoulders. Daydreams were all very well, but she needed to have a talk with Dr Joshua Kent and find out just what sort of arrangements she would need to make for him now that he was out of commission.

She didn't even have any idea where he worked, nor whether he'd thought of contacting them to tell them about his accident. Nor did she know whether there were other family members who would want to know—his parents, perhaps.

First things first, though. She needed a telephone.

'Could I use your phone to call my hotel?' she asked as soon as she entered his room to collect the tray.

'Of course.' He reached out to the instrument on the cabinet beside his bed. 'I'm sure you'll be far more comfortable there, and you needn't worry about the two of us—Molly'll be back in the morning. I'm only sorry that your evening has been hijacked like this. Your time in Cornwall is turning into a real bus-man's holiday.'

'I don't mind—it's not as if I had anything desperately interesting planned,' she said dismissively. 'Anyway, I'm just going to let the hotel know that I won't be coming back tonight at all. I said I was going to be doing your observations tonight, and I will.'

'I don't really think that's necessary,' he began, then, when he caught sight of the expression on Bethan's face, suddenly stopped speaking.

At first Bethan was hurt that he was rejecting her help, but suddenly she realised that it was his pride which was making him object rather than his common sense.

'Dr Kent,' she said, copying his dispassionate delivery exactly. 'I think it's *entirely* necessary—for your daughter's sake, if not your own. If there were some sort of emergency, how on earth would you get yourself out, never mind save Sam's life?

'Apart from which,' she continued swiftly when it looked as if he was going to interrupt, 'it's quite possible that she's going to need to go to the bathroom at least once and possibly more often before Molly returns. Are you willing to put her recovery back, by forcing her to do more than she's ready for?'

He put one hand up, just like a child in school, asking permission to speak.

'I'd already come to those conclusions myself,' he admitted quietly. 'It goes against the grain to have to rely on others, but I could never jeopardise Sam.'

'Then...why did you try to interrupt?'

'Actually, all I was going to do was ask you to call

me Josh. It seems a little over-formal to call me Dr
Kent when you've peeled me up off my bathroom
floor with my trousers round my ankles.'

Bethan laughed, but she wished he hadn't brought
that particular event up. She'd been trying very hard
to forget how much she'd seen of him—and the fact
that all of it was now hidden just an arm's length
away under the bedclothes.

Although she'd used his given name when she was
trying to rouse him while he was trapped in his car,
the thought of calling him Josh suddenly seemed too
intimate in the confines of his own bedroom—but
how could she refuse without offering a reason?

'Well, ah...Josh,' she said, reluctantly using his
first name, 'are you ready for your next dose of painkillers?'

'Oh, it's not so bad,' he said dismissively.

'Mr Macho, eh?' she teased.

'*Dr* Macho, please!' he corrected with a smile that
nearly stopped her heart.

When she'd managed to unstick her tongue from
the roof of her mouth she knew the only way she
wasn't going to make a complete fool of herself was
if she continued to joke with him.

'I bet you're one of those doctors who never likes
taking medication unless they're absolutely dying.'

'Got it in one,' he said wryly. 'And I thought the
stiff upper lip made us inscrutable.'

'We'll see how inscrutable you are when everything wears off in the wee small hours,' Bethan ban-
tered. 'Still, I'll be checking up on you every hour,
so if you change your mind just let me know.'

She'd turned to leave the room when he called her
back.

'Open the second drawer down,' he suggested,

pointing to the beautiful old mahogany military chest on the other side of the room, the brass corners and recessed handles gleaming softly with years of use. 'There's a pile of T-shirts in there. Help yourself to one—it'll be more comfortable than sleeping in your underwear.'

Bethan could have cursed her lack of experience when she felt the heat sweep up her throat into her face, and she whirled away to hide her reaction, hoping that he hadn't noticed.

What on earth would he think if he realised that just the thought of wearing his clothing against her naked body was enough to cause her brain to short-circuit?

She grabbed the first one to hand and threw him a 'goodnight' over her shoulder before she escaped towards the bathroom.

Sam's screams woke Bethan from a sound sleep and she sat up, wondering what on earth was going on. It was the same groggy feeling she remembered from the dark days of her training when one day seemed to merge into the next without any discernible break, and for a moment she thought she was still in the middle of it.

Then Sam cried out again and, remembering where she was, Bethan swung her feet out onto the floor.

'Hang on, sweetheart, I'm coming,' she called, not knowing whether the child would be able to hear her through her fear.

She hurried along the landing and into her room, not bothering to pause to find light switches in her urgency to reach her.

'I'm here, Sam. I'm here,' she crooned as she gathered the shaking youngster into her arms and began to rock her. 'You're safe, sweetheart. I've got you.'

The screaming stopped as soon as Bethan pulled her onto her lap, but it took a long time before she stopped crying and even longer before the shaking died away.

'B-Bethan...?' Sam hiccuped as she buried her face against the borrowed T-shirt. 'My mummy died.'

'Did she, sweetheart?' Bethan said, hoping her voice remained calm in spite of her shock. She didn't know why, but she'd been so certain that Sam's parents were divorced...

'A car hit her and she b-bumped her head and then she died,' Sam continued with heartbreaking simplicity.

'I'm sorry,' Bethan murmured, thinking once again how totally inadequate those words were to express so much emotion.

'It hit my leg and broke the bone all to p-pieces,' she added without a trace of self-pity, and was silent for some while.

Bethan sat quietly, holding her close and rocking her as if she were a much younger child, instinctively feeling that she needed the physical contact.

She was quiet for so long that Bethan was beginning to think that she'd fallen asleep again, but suddenly she spoke again.

'Is...is my daddy going to die?' she whispered into the dark silence. 'He hit his head and it was bleeding and then he couldn't talk to me for a long time...and...and...'

'No, Sam,' Bethan said quickly, her heart going out to the terrified child. 'Oh, sweetheart, no, he's not going to die. He's just hurt his knee and bumped his head, and when all the bruises have gone he'll be as good as new.'

'P-promise?' Sam begged, her little chin wobbling.

'I promise,' she said. 'Now, how about peeping into his room to see if he's being a good boy, and then you can go back to sleep?'

'Yes, please.'

Bethan cradled the little girl on one hip, and just before she pushed Josh's door open put one finger to her lips.

'Don't make a noise or you might wake him up,' she whispered.

Sam nodded, her dark blue eyes very serious as she gazed across at the man sprawled on the bed. He looked peaceful, the lean planes of his face lit by the shaded lamp Bethan had left switched on so that she could do her observations without disturbing his sleep too much.

Josh was naked almost to the waist, and had turned so that Bethan could clearly see the huge bruise on his shoulder where the point of impact must have been greatest when the car had turned over.

She'd been surprised that such an athletic-looking man had been so slow to master his crutches, but once she'd seen the extent of the bruising she'd realised that it was no wonder he'd been having trouble coping with them if one of his shoulders was this badly bruised.

The book he'd been reading was still lying open by one hand on top of the bedclothes, one long finger trapped between the pages as though to mark his place.

'OK?' Bethan whispered, dragging her eyes away to look down at her little passenger.

'OK,' Sam answered with a nod, quite happy now to be tucked back into bed.

Bethan was making her way back to her own room, desperate for just a little more sleep, when she heard a noise in Josh's room. A quick glance at her watch told her it was about time she checked up on him anyway, and she gave a tired sigh as she pushed the door open.

'What are you doing?' she demanded softly when she saw him sitting on the edge of his bed, his injured leg sticking out stiffly under the restriction of the heavy strapping.

'I was trying to work out how I was going to get to my crutches,' he said with a scowl. 'You left them in the wrong place.'

'No, I didn't,' she contradicted, and planted one fist militantly on each hip. 'You're not supposed to be galloping about—that's why *I'm* here. If you want anything I can bring it to you.'

'Not everything,' he grumbled wryly, his cheek-bones colouring endearingly. 'I need the bathroom.'

'Ah...'

Bethan felt her own cheeks grow warm and busied herself with fetching the crutches for him. Even if she'd had a bottle or a bedpan for him to use, she had a feeling that he'd have refused. For some reason she was convinced that he'd rather crawl over broken glass than have her perform any intimate functions for him.

She suddenly remembered the bottle of painkillers the harassed young doctor had handed her on their way out of the hospital and went back to her room to retrieve them from her handbag. For a moment she paused in thought about where she should put them— far enough away that she could have control of the dosage or close enough that he could take too many—then chastised herself.

'He's a doctor, for heaven's sake,' she muttered as she put the tablets on the bedside cabinet. 'He knows what he's doing with painkillers—with his aversion to medication, he's hardly likely to overdose himself.'

Bethan heard the sound of running water from along the corridor when she returned from a quick trip to the kitchen with a jug of water and a glass.

She decided there would be nothing wrong with waiting to see that Josh got back to bed safely and busied herself by straightening his bed while she waited for him to return. She was just bending to tuck the dangling corner of the bedspread out of his way when she heard the rhythmic thump of his crutches.

It was the hiss of his indrawn breath in the doorway that made her whirl to face him, and when she found his gaze riveted on the hem of the T-shirt she'd borrowed from him she suddenly realised that her activities had caused it to ride right up.

Bethan grabbed for the hem and yanked it down to mid-thigh level again.

She'd totally forgotten what she was wearing until that second, and the stunned expression on his face suddenly told her that she might have been showing him rather more of her body than she wanted.

As he stumped his way across to the bed she waited for the crippling wash of embarrassment to flood over her, but was stunned to feel a totally unaccustomed twist of excitement deep inside.

'Do...do you want anything?' she stammered, her mind only half on her words as she tried to fathom her strange reaction towards this man. Josh made a strangled sound and she suddenly realised how her words sounded.

'I mean...do you need anything...any more pain-killer?' She finally stumbled to a halt with a gesture towards the small bottle on his bedside cabinet.

'I hate the way those things make me feel,' he grumbled as he lowered himself gingerly to the edge of the bed. 'I don't like being out of control...but the damn thing aches like fury so I'm going to have to take them if I'm going to get any sleep.'

Bethan relieved him of the crutches and lifted the covers aside so that he could slide his legs into bed.

'Well, if there's nothing I can get you...' she said as she propped the crutches against the wall beside the military chest again. She turned to leave his room, loath to go back to the solitude of her own, knowing that he was in pain.

If she was honest with herself, she'd discovered that she was reluctant to waste any of this night in sleep.

She had no idea why she found this man so fasci-nating—why she'd felt so drawn to him right from the first time she'd seen him—but something inside her didn't want to lose a single second of their brief time together.

'Bethan...wait.'

Josh called her back and she had the strange feeling that he was as reluctant as she was to end their time together.

'Are you very tired?' he asked when she turned back to face him from the doorway. 'Or would you be willing to keep me company for a while—just until the painkillers kick in?'

'I don't mind,' she said, with what she hoped was a casual nonchalance—anything to hide the way her pulse rate had suddenly doubled.

He was silent while she sat on the side of his bed

and self-consciously pulled the hem of the T-shirt down to cover a little more of her thighs. Not that she was ashamed of them—the amount of exercise she got, working in A and E, seemed to burn up the calories—she'd certainly lost the few spare inches she'd had when she joined the unit.

The small amount of walking she'd done up on the moors since she'd come down to Cornwall had even given her the slight golden start of a tan...

'I heard you talking to Sam,' he said suddenly, drawing her eyes up to meet his in the muted light.

She saw the shadow of pain on his face and when she heard him draw in a deep breath she wondered what was coming next.

'Sam *saw* her mother die,' he said bluntly, as though spitting out the fact like an unpalatable mouthful. 'Livvy hit her head on the pavement and fractured her skull. It was a hit and run by an underage driver— just twelve years old...'

Bethan couldn't imagine what he'd gone through to lose his wife like that and then to have to cope with...

'Is that when Sam's leg was injured?' she asked, putting facts together in her head.

'Yes. Her mother tried to shelter her with her own body, but she fell on her and both the bones in Sam's lower leg were completely shattered.'

'You said she'd had her last operation recently. How many has it taken to get her this far?'

'Too many,' he said bleakly. 'At first they thought the nerves and blood supply were too badly damaged to bother trying to save it, but they took a chance. Then one bone refused to mend and they ended up having to plate bone grafts in position while they held the other together with external fixators.'

'And the most recent episode?' Bethan could only imagine the amount of pain that little child had suffered—as if losing her mother hadn't been bad enough.

'They were getting rid of all the temporary hardware,' he said succinctly. 'She's got an appointment soon when they'll tell her whether she's ready to get rid of her crutches.' He laughed briefly. 'She's a real daredevil on them—unlike me. She's really going to enjoy seeing me hobble around tomorrow.'

Bethan smiled. 'She's a smashing kid, and she obviously loves her daddy.'

'When there's only the two of you, you have to take care of each other,' he said simply. 'In the space of one terrible moment, she went from being a healthy little girl with two parents to being severely injured—possibly disabled for life—with no mother to comfort her and no little brother or sister to take her mind off things during the months she was confined to bed.'

The thought of all that Josh and his daughter had lost was like a heavy weight inside her chest, but something about the words he'd used had her looking up at him with a question on the tip of her tongue.

It was almost as if he'd been waiting for her to make the connection because he nodded.

'We'd never intended for Sam to be an only child and the next baby was already on the way when Livvy died. She was nearly five months pregnant.'

'Oh, Josh…'

For the first time his name didn't feel awkward as she reached out her hand towards him, everything inside her wanting to offer him comfort when she saw the bleak anguish in his eyes.

'I can't imagine…' she began, then had to stop and bite her lip as her throat closed up. Even that didn't prevent the tears of sympathy from spilling over to trickle down her cheeks.

'Ah, Bethan, don't cry. You're too soft-hearted for your own good,' he murmured huskily as he reached for her and pulled her into his arms, cradling her against the warmth of his naked chest.

CHAPTER FIVE

'JOSH!' Bethan murmured through her tears, shocked to find herself wrapped in his arms, but then she realised that there was nowhere else that she would rather be and subsided against the comforting warmth of him.

It felt so good, so right to be here like this with him, with her head tucked into the crook of his neck and her hand splayed over his naked chest where his heart beat out its heavy rhythm.

It felt as if he surrounded her protectively, and as she breathed she drew in the indefinable mixture of soap and warm male flesh that seemed to belong only to him—a mixture that seemed to stir her to her depths with unnamed longings.

'Bethan?' he murmured when she grew still, and lifted her chin with gentle fingers to persuade her to meet his eyes.

Bethan raised her lids shyly and could have drowned in the deep blue which gazed down at her.

Suddenly heat flooded through her and she knew that she was where she was meant to be.

All her doubts and fears disappeared as if they had never existed, and as his head angled towards hers the echo of her grandmother's voice faded away into the distance.

She had felt the electricity between them when she'd kissed him at the scene of the accident, but that had been a mere tingle in comparison with the lightning bolt that struck her when he took possession of her mouth.

Unlike lightning, the charge between them just seemed to increase with each new contact, each new depth, until she had to wrench her mouth away just to draw breath.

'Oh, God, Bethan, I need you,' Josh murmured hoarsely, his own breathing rough and laboured. His hands explored her body feverishly, quickly finding the hem of the T-shirt he'd lent her and sliding underneath to palm the soft curves of her bottom.

'I nearly died on the spot when I saw these peeping at me when you were making the bed,' he confided as he kneaded and shaped them. 'All I could think about was how much I wanted to see all of you...'

He started to slide his hands up her back, gathering the fabric as he went.

Bethan shivered as every nerve ending he touched went on the alert, and she suddenly realised that he wanted to take it off her.

'I didn't have any extra clothing with me,' she began as nervousness suddenly took hold of her tongue and she hurried to excuse her lack of clothing. 'I'll have to wear the same clothes in the morning so I washed out my underwear and—'

'And hung it over the top of the shower door to drive me crazy,' he finished with a growl. 'I came back along the landing, knowing that you weren't wearing anything under the T-shirt...' His voice stopped as he stripped the makeshift nightshirt over her head and dropped it over the side of the bed, his eyes riveted on her naked body.

'Ah, Bethan, how can you possibly be more beautiful than I imagined?' he whispered.

His hands outlined her shoulders while his eyes

seared her everywhere they touched—and they touched her everywhere.

First the pale creamy globes of her breasts which seemed to tingle and grow heavy as he gazed at them, her nipples tightening in expectation as he cupped her in his warm hands.

By the time he reached the slender curve of her waist and slid one hand down to cover the dark triangle at the juncture of her thighs, the secrets hidden there had grown swollen and moist.

Every nerve in her body was drawn tight with anticipation and she couldn't help the soft moan which escaped her when he touched her there for the first time, her legs parting helplessly to allow him to explore.

'Touch me, Bethan,' he murmured hoarsely as he took her hand and pressed it against his chest. 'I need to feel your hands on me too.'

Tentatively, Bethan ran her fingers through the silky whorls of hair, revelling in the way she made him gasp when she accidentally flicked the tiny bud of his nipple.

'Oh, God, yes,' he groaned, and mimicked the movement for her.

She gasped when she felt the sharp response deep inside herself, marvelling that stimulation of her nipple could reach as far as her womb.

'You like it too?' he demanded as he did it again. 'And how about this?' He bent to take her nipple into his mouth and suckled her like a hungry baby at the breast.

'Yes-s-s,' she hissed, and arched towards him, unconsciously offering herself to his ministrations.

'God, you're so responsive,' he groaned, pressing his face against her while he fought for breath. 'I'm sorry, Bethan, but I don't know if I can wait much longer.'

He lifted his head and gazed straight at her, the flush of arousal along his cheekbones growing darker as he seemed to fight an internal battle.

'I... It's been a long time for me,' he said in a low voice. 'I don't know if I'll be much use to you... The way I feel at the moment, I'll probably explode as soon as I get near you.'

Bethan felt a quiver of apprehension at the thought of what they were about to do, but when she looked into his eyes and saw the depth of his need there was no way she could deny him.

Wordlessly, she cupped her hand around his face and brought his lips to hers for the merest hint of a kiss, then slid to one side to pull the bedclothes out of the way.

'Oh.' She swallowed dryly when she saw the evidence of the extent of his arousal, even though he was still in his underwear.

'I'll need a little help, getting rid of those,' he murmured with a hint of laughter in his voice. 'The way I was feeling when I saw those lacy scraps of nothing in the bathroom I didn't dare try to take them off myself.'

'Then allow me,' she offered with a sudden surge of boldness. 'After all, it *is* partly my fault you're in this condition, even though I had nothing to do with the state of your knee.'

She slid her hands under the edge of the elastic and lifted it carefully away from him before she began to pull his pants down his body.

He moaned and she froze.

'Did I hurt your knee?' she demanded, and he chuckled.

'Not my knee, no. The pain's a little higher up and it's not getting any better when I can see this tantalising view again.' As he spoke he ran his hand over the curve of her bottom.

She hadn't realised that when she turned away from him to pull his pants down he would be looking at her naked body, and she felt the wash of heat travel up her throat and into her face.

'You aren't shy, are you?' he teased gently, and pulled her up to lie beside him on the bed.

'In spite of the fact that I've seen hundreds, maybe thousands of naked men, yes, I'm still a bit shy,' she admitted softly. 'Blame it on my grandmother—she's the one who brought me up.'

'Well, I find it incredibly arousing,' he confided, his deep voice taking on a huskier note as he rolled onto his side and ran a caressing hand over her. 'A fact of which you've just had ample evidence.'

Bethan drew in a little gasp when his hand reached her soft curls and began to explore again.

In no time at all she was nearly mindless with arousal and willingly parted her legs further when he pressed his thigh between them.

'Ah-h, damn,' he gasped between gritted teeth, and slumped onto his back. 'I forgot about my knee.'

'Oh, Josh,' she exclaimed with sudden guilt. 'Did you do it any further damage? What do you want me to do?'

'Bury me,' he groaned dramatically. 'I think I'm going to die of frustration.'

Bethan pressed her lips tightly together but couldn't stop her laughter escaping.

'I don't know what you're laughing about,' he growled menacingly as he caught hold of her hand. 'By the time you've finished you won't have the

breath left to blow out a candle, let alone laugh...'
And before she realised what he intended to do he
had pulled her over on top of him.

'Josh!' she squeaked, startled by the unexpected
position, and tried to slither off

'Oh, no, you don't, woman,' he said as he circled
her waist with both hands and held her in place. 'According to some people or other—Chinese, I think—
you saved my life so you're now responsible for it.
You can't let me die now when the remedy is in your
hands.'

There was life and laughter in his eyes, the deep
blue gleaming up at her as he spouted his nonsense,
and suddenly Bethan realised that there was nothing
to fear—not with Josh.

'So what is your pleasure, sir?' she murmured as
she braced her hands on his chest and pushed herself
up into a sitting position.

She saw the way his eyes were drawn to her
breasts, and all of a sudden the fact that they were
naked to his gaze became something to revel in.

'Do you like what you see, sir?' she purred, amazed
that she was able to tease him this way when she'd
never done anything like it in her life before.

She ran her fingers through her hair and arched her
back and suddenly realised that the jolt to his knee
had done nothing to diminish the strength of Josh's
arousal.

One last flicker of self-doubt had her drawing in a
deep breath for courage before she slid a little further
down his body.

'I think...' She paused and wet her lips with a nervous tongue, hoping that he would take her hesitation
for teasing rather than lack of experience. 'I think I
might need just a little bit of...co-operation at this

point,' she said, her voice dying away to a whisper as he wordlessly complied.

'Bethan…!' he groaned as she sank onto him, his voice drowning out her whimper as she felt him burst his way through the hidden evidence of her innocence.

Her muscles clenched tight against the intrusion and she froze, scared that the pain would grow unbearable if she dared to stir.

'Stay still a moment,' Josh said through gritted teeth, his hands spanning her waist as he lay with his head thrown back and his eyes clenched tightly shut as though in mortal agony. 'I'm sorry, but if you move now it'll be all over.'

Bethan drew in a shaky breath and wondered how on earth she was going to break the news to him that she couldn't bear for this to go any further.

She knew it was her own fault—she should have told him that she'd never done this before, but she honestly hadn't expected him—it—to feel so…so big.

'Hey, relax,' he said, his voice a soft caress, and she saw that his eyes had opened and he was looking up at her—knew he must be seeing her discomfort on her face.

'I don't know what… Do you want…? Would you rather I got off?' she stammered, half hoping that he'd agree so that she didn't have to confess her inadequacy.

'No! God, no, I couldn't bear it—it feels so good. Just give me a minute,' he said quickly, tightening his grip on her as though afraid she would leave him. 'I never expected it to be quite so…intense…so incredibly…incredible.'

His incoherence was so endearing that Bethan felt the unfurling of the first sweet tendrils of pride in her femininity and couldn't stop the start of a smug smile curving the corners of her mouth.

Suddenly she realised that, by thinking about what Josh had said and what he was feeling, she had allowed her muscles to relax and the pain had gone. All she was left with was an awe-inspiring impression of fullness and a wonderful feeling of rightness that an elemental part of Josh was actually inside her body.

Then it wasn't enough just to passively accept his presence inside her—she was consumed with the need to move.

'What are you doing, woman?' he growled when she experimentally tightened her inner muscles around him, and she couldn't help a smile of delight when she realised that alternately clenching and releasing them not only increased the depth of his penetration inside her but also made him groan aloud.

Soon surreptitious movement wasn't enough and she began to rock, tentatively at first while she found out what felt best, then more firmly when her body took over control of her actions.

Before she'd realised what was happening to her she was moving faster and faster as a strange tension started to coil tighter and tighter inside until, with an explosion of sensation like the brightest supernova in the sky, she collapsed bonelessly on his chest.

It was some time before either of them had enough breath to form a word, never mind a coherent sentence.

'Just a quiet funeral will do,' he said, his voice a deep rumble under her ear.

Bethan chuckled weakly.

'You'll have to wait a year or two while I summon up the energy,' she murmured.

'I don't mind waiting.' His deep voice sounded lazy as it stroked its way along her nerves and felt nearly as sexy as the fingers stroking rhythmically up and down her back and hips.

She stretched like a pampered cat and realised that they were still intimately joined.

'I'll give you until the next century to stop moving like that,' he murmured, but there was a distinctly drowsy sound to his voice.

Bethan lay still for a moment and listened to the sound of his breathing change. As his hand gradually stopped its soothing movement she realised that, thanks to a combination of exhaustion, painkillers and the oldest insomnia remedy in the world, he had finally fallen asleep.

Bethan groaned when she surfaced to the sound of a phone ringing, then sat bolt upright in the bed when she opened her eyes and didn't recognise any of her surroundings.

'Where am I?' she muttered as she swung her feet over the edge of the bed and winced at an unexpected soreness.

Suddenly she knew exactly where she was and a wave of heat enveloped her at the memory of what had happened last night.

The strident sound of the phone continued to jar on her nerves and she realised that she was probably the only person in the house fit enough to answer it.

When she'd left Josh's room last night she'd borrowed a shirt from his wardrobe to cover the skimpy T-shirt.

She grabbed for the shirt now and thrust her arms into the sleeves, but while she was still crossing the room the ringing stopped.

'Dr Josh,' called a female voice, just as Bethan reached out to pull her door open, and she stopped in surprise. There was somebody else in the house...

'Dr Josh, will you answer the phone?' the voice called, louder this time. 'It's Mrs Pengelly for an appointment.'

It didn't sound as if she was going to come up the stairs so Bethan cautiously stuck her head out, then stepped forward to the banisters.

'Hello?' Bethan called. 'Who's there?' A tightly permed head of grey hair appeared below.

'And who are you?' the lady demanded in return. 'What are you doing in the doctor's house?'

'I drove him back from the hospital last night,' Bethan explained. 'His car was written off in the accident.'

'Accident?' The poor woman was obviously horrified. 'What accident? Did something happen to Sam?'

'Sam's fine but Josh hurt his knee,' she began, cutting the explanation short when there was a bellow from Josh's room.

'Bethan! Get in here quickly. I need those wretched crutches.'

'To hear is to obey,' Bethan quipped with a wry expression, and was rewarded by a chuckle from the woman below.

'Sounds as if you've got the measure of him already,' she said. 'I'm Molly Wonnacott, and you're...?'

'Dammit!' Josh roared, interrupting her introduction. 'Either get my crutches or bring me the phone and the appointment book...somebody!'

'I'll bring the book,' Molly called as she disappeared from sight. 'The phone's in his room.'

'*There* you are,' Josh growled from the edge of his bed, his hair standing up on end and a villainous stubble shadowing his jaw. 'Why do you keep putting the damn crutches on the other side of the room? And you moved the phone. How am I supposed to reach them?'

'You aren't,' she retorted. 'The crutches, that is. Not without supervision for the next twenty-four hours at least. And a good morning to you, too,' she added facetiously.

'You must be joking!' he said, utterly incensed. 'How am I supposed to get about? I've got a job to do. We're not all on holiday, you know.'

'I also know that if you don't treat that knee right you'll be piling up trouble for yourself in the future,' she retorted, equally heatedly. 'You know as well as I do that it will take a heck of a lot longer to get back on your feet after a knee-joint replacement than the couple of days you spend now.'

'It's all very well for you to stand there, sermonising, but I've got a patient waiting to speak to me on the other end of that phone—or are you going to stop me talking to her?'

Bethan passed the phone to him without another word, then stepped aside when his door swung open and Molly appeared with the appointment book in her hand.

'Here you are,' she muttered as she thrust the book at Bethan. 'Rather you than me when he's in this sort of mood! I'll go and see to Sam.'

'No, Mrs Pengelly,' Josh was saying when Bethan tuned in to him again. 'You haven't rung too early, but I'm afraid I can't get out to see you this morning. If you can't get someone to bring you to the surgery you'll have to wait until I can get to you.'

The voice on the other end of the line sounded like an extremely angry wasp and she saw Josh draw in a deep breath, seeming to pray for patience while he waited for a chance to interrupt.

He glanced across at Bethan, signalled for her to open the book at the appropriate page and glanced down at the list of appointments already booked.

'Well, then,' he said, finally having to speak over her complaining voice. 'I'll expect to see you at half past ten. And, don't forget, if you can't make the appointment, ring up and let me know so that I can give it to someone else.'

He put the phone down with rather more force than necessary and held his hand out for the appointment book, but Bethan had made herself comfortable on the end of his bed and had already printed the woman's name neatly against the ten-thirty slot.

'Are you really intending to take a full morning's surgery?' she demanded when she saw that, with one small gap in the middle, the list went on to nearly twelve. 'Couldn't one of your partners cover for you in the circumstances?'

'If I had a partner available he probably would, but as I haven't…'

'No partner? At all?' she demanded, horrified. 'Who did your night visits last night? Who does the weekends?'

She saw the way he pressed his lips together and realised he wasn't going to answer. He was probably thinking it was none of her business, she admitted silently.

'How long have you been coping like this?' she challenged, her concern for this stubborn man over-riding her wish to respect his privacy, but the phone rang again and he grabbed for it.

'Pendruccombe Surgery,' he said, sounding almost relieved not to have to answer her question.

Bethan mentally threw her hands up in the air and turned to leave the room. She had an idea she'd get far more answers out of Molly.

She found Molly in Sam's room, just fastening an extra knot on the laces of her diminutive trainers.

'G'morning, Bethan,' the little girl said with a wide smile when she caught sight of her over Molly's shoulder. 'I'd forgotten you were here.'

'Good morning, Sam-*antha*,' she teased, glad to see that yesterday's events didn't seem to have stopped Sam from sleeping well and waking up cheerful. 'I gave you and your daddy a ride home in my car last night, but you were fast asleep and didn't know a thing about it until I carried you to the bathroom.'

'Is Daddy's car still broken?' Sam asked with a frown. 'Will the garage be able to fix it?'

'I don't know, sweetheart. He'll probably be able to find out later on today.'

'If he hasn't got a car, how will he get to the sick people?' she demanded, obviously bright enough to grasp the immediate problems that a lack of transport would cause her father.

'How about having some breakfast and asking him all these questions afterwards?' Molly suggested, and held her arms out to the youngster.

'Are you having breakfast with us, too?' Sam demanded chirpily. 'Molly will cook you something if you ask her.'

'I'd love to have some breakfast, but I need to get dressed first. Shall I see you when I get downstairs?'

'OK,' she agreed cheerfully, and tightened her arm around Molly Wonnacott's shoulder as Molly lifted her.

'Oh, before you go...' Bethan bit her lip as she tried to sort out the things she needed to know before she could tackle Josh on a firm footing. 'Isn't there someone who could take over the practice for a few days to allow Josh's knee to recover? He shouldn't really be putting it under stress while it's all bruised and swollen.'

'He should have, but...' The woman cast a glance towards the room next door when the phone rang again. 'There are three of them altogether, but Tim's away on his honeymoon and Martin...well, he's on sick leave.'

'Is there any chance he's recovered enough to be able to come back to cover for Josh?' Bethan asked, frustrated that the poor woman seemed to be hiding something from her when all she wanted to do was help.

Molly bit her lip in indecision, obviously hating the thought that anyone might think she was a gossip, then blurted out in a rush, 'Between you and me, it isn't likely that he'll be back at all.'

'Oh, but—' Bethan began, only to be interrupted by Sam.

'Uncle Martin's a 'holic and he's gone to get dry,' she announced with the air of imparting an important secret. 'I'm not s'posed to know but I heard someone talking 'bout him. Bethan, what's a 'holic and how did he get wet? He doesn't even like swimming.'

Bethan laughed as Molly whisked Sam away, but she really felt like crying.

No wonder the poor man was so exhausted... It looked as if he'd been trying to run a three-man practice all by himself for...how long? What was going to happen now *he* was the one who needed time off from work?

'Bethan?' he shouted, frustration evident in his voice. 'Where are you, woman?'

She stood for a minute in the empty room and closed her eyes, remembering the husky tone of his deep voice when he'd been murmuring compliments, his hands stroking her and exploring her as she'd never allowed another man to do.

When she'd slid out of his bed last night she'd actually stood looking down at him, wondering what on earth was different about this man.

She couldn't be in love with him—she'd only met the man a few hours ago, for heaven's sake. But if it wasn't love, what were these feelings...so strong that for the first time she had totally ignored the basic tenets of her upbringing?

When she'd pulled the covers over his naked body and left him sprawled across the bed with his handsome face relaxed in sleep, she'd tried to guess what they would say to each other when they came face to face in the morning.

In the end, she'd decided that there were two main possibilities.

He would either approach the whole thing in a very logical way and suggest that, as it had only happened in the heat of the moment, it was better forgotten, or he would propose that they treated the whole situation as a holiday fling and enjoy it while it lasted.

The last thing she had expected was that he would act as if the most magical event of her life had never happened.

'Bethan?' he called again, breaking into her despondent musings, this time his voice sounding almost desperate. 'Look, I'm sorry I shouted but...I need to go to the bathroom...'

'From the sublime to the prosaic,' Bethan muttered

as she hurried out of Sam's room and pushed Josh's door open.

Wordlessly she retrieved his crutches and handed them to him, relieving him of the appointment book and pen before they tipped off the edge of the bed as he levered himself to his feet.

He paused in the doorway and looked back over his shoulder, apparently totally unconcerned that he was as naked as the day he was born.

'If there are any calls while I'm in there could you tell them—'

'I can make an educated guess,' Bethan broke in, studiously fixing her eyes on the open page, after her hungry gaze had devoured the lean perfection of his back and the tight curves of his buttocks on his way across the room.

She'd only just managed to force herself to drag her eyes away from him in time when he'd looked back at her, and now all she wanted him to do was take temptation out of her sight.

The phone rang twice before he returned, and each time she took the name and telephone number and promised that the call would be returned as soon as possible.

She'd just put the phone down after the second call when he returned to the room, this time wearing the dark blue towelling robe she'd seen hanging on the back of the bathroom door.

The colour almost exactly matched his eyes but it was the dark colour staining his cheeks that caught her attention.

'Why didn't you say something when I went marching out of here without any clothing on?' he growled, obviously too embarrassed to meet her eyes.

'Why should I?' she asked, proud that she sounded

so calm, and suddenly saw a way to wring a reaction out of him about their explosive liaison last night. 'After all,' she added, almost as an afterthought, 'you weren't showing me anything I hadn't already seen.'

'That's hardly the point,' he said. 'I don't usually go parading around naked in front of near-strangers.'

'I'm pleased to hear it,' she said sweetly, 'especially with an impressionable little girl in the house.'

'You know what I mean,' he began heatedly as the phone began to ring again. 'Dammit,' he muttered, and held his hand out for the receiver.

Bethan stayed him with an upraised hand and answered it herself.

'Pendruccombe Surgery. Can I help you?' she said, and bit back a smile when there was a pause on the other end.

'Is the doctor there today?' quavered an elderly voice. 'I need someone to cut my toenails. They're so long I can nearly climb trees.'

Bethan couldn't help chuckling at the image.

'Well, if you'd like to give me your name and telephone number I'll make certain that somebody calls you back—just in case a dog barks and you take off in a fright.'

'I could have taken that,' Josh pointed out when she finished.

'You could also do something about getting dressed,' she retorted. 'It's almost eight o'clock and, according to this book, your first patient is booked in for half past. I don't know how far you have to travel to get to work, but that leaves you very little time to eat and get yourself ready to go.'

'Then it's a good job that the surgery is in the house, isn't it?' he returned smartly as he stomped across to his wardrobe and balanced on one crutch while he grabbed a clean shirt.

'How many staff do you have and what time will they arrive?' she demanded as she flicked through the appointment book, ostensibly looking for information but in reality trying to occupy her eyes so that she wouldn't be caught ogling him.

'Two part-time receptionists, a full-time practice nurse and two community nurses. We also share several other staff within a group of practices—like the chiropodist and the speech therapist...'

The sound of muttered swearing alerted her that all was not well, although she was certain he would rather she ignored him and would never actually *ask* for help.

'If you sit down on the side of the bed I can make that job much easier,' she offered, tucking the pen in the book to mark the page before she put it aside.

'I can manage,' he said with a stubborn lift to his chin.

'I'm sure you can...eventually,' she agreed. 'But those patients will be arriving *before* Christmas.'

Bethan had to hide her smile when he sighed heavily and subsided onto the bed. It was the way he made certain that he'd wrapped his robe modestly across his lap that amused her most, but he submitted silently to having first his underwear and then his trousers threaded onto his feet and pulled up as far as his knees. Even so, she could almost *feel* his frustration radiating towards her.

'I suppose you've explored the possibility of getting in a locum?'

'Without success,' Josh said with weary resignation. 'There are too few to go around, and none who wanted to come this far from civilisation, in spite of being offered an arm and a leg to do it.'

'There must be *something* you can do,' she declared heatedly as she straightened. 'You can't be expected to be on call twenty-four hours a day, seven days a week. You had your accident because you were too tired to concentrate. At this rate, you'll be so exhausted that you really *will* kill yourself...or a patient.'

CHAPTER SIX

JOSH glared at Bethan, but before he could speak the phone rang again.

Bethan reached for it with an answering glare in his direction and proceeded to book a patient for an appointment the following day.

'Why didn't you book her into the gap at eleven today?' he demanded, pointing to the empty space on the page. 'I could have seen her then.'

'Two reasons,' she replied crisply. 'Firstly, she was a non-urgent case—just a routine annual check-up before you give her the next prescription for her hormone replacement therapy. She's got two weeks of tablets left so there's no hurry. Secondly, that space is having *your* name written in it.'

'What on earth for?' he demanded crossly.

'For your treatment,' she said as she printed his name neatly in the space.

'*What* treatment?'

'On your knee, of course.' She closed the book with a snap.

She was too tired after a long disturbed night of getting up to peer into his eyes to make sure he wasn't suffering delayed reaction to his head injury to put up with any obstreperousness from him.

'You know as well as I do that it needs passive mobilisation at intervals or the whole joint will stiffen up. I've already checked that there's some ice in the freezer and I'll arrange for Molly to make some more.'

'Bossy nurses,' he huffed, a deep scowl on his face. 'And *you're* bossy enough to be a doctor!'

'That could be because I *am* a doctor,' she said with a smug smile and watched his jaw drop.

'What? But... At the show you and Jane were talking about...'

'About doing our training at the same hospital,' she finished with a nod. 'We did, but not in the same discipline. I'm actually working in A and E at the moment but I still remember enough about my time in Orthopaedics to know what I'm talking about.'

She thoroughly enjoyed watching the confusion on his face while he assimilated the facts. She'd had the feeling that he'd thought she was a nurse, but until the last few minutes it hadn't really mattered.

She heard Sam's voice downstairs and realised that she'd spent enough time gloating.

'You'd better finish dressing and get downstairs for some breakfast before the practice opens,' she said. 'If that book and the way the phone's been ringing are any indication you might not have another chance to stoke up your boiler for some time.'

He nodded absently, his eyes fixed on her under darkly frowning brows as she left him to it.

She took a rapid shower and leapt into her clean underwear before she hurried back to her room and donned the rest of her clothes.

A glance in the mirror told her that in spite of hanging them up carefully last night they were still a little the worse for wear after the events of yesterday, but until she had a chance to go to her hotel they would have to do.

Josh's shoulder must still have been painful because he was less than smoothly proficient on his

crutches when they joined Sam in the kitchen, Bethan
carrying the all-important appointment book.

'Daddy! You got some too!' Sam crowed when she
saw him hobbling in. 'Now we can be twins!'

Bethan looked from the petite little girl to her tall
muscular father and had to fight the urge to laugh at
the image.

'Perhaps the two of you can have a race,' she suggested, making him pause with his mug of coffee half-
way to his mouth.

'Race?' he repeated warily.

'Yes. To see which one of you can get better first,'
Bethan explained. 'You said that Sam's appointment
is on Monday to see if she can go without them.'

'That's right, but—'

'Then Sam will have to remind you to do your exercises when she does hers so that you don't get left
behind.'

Gotcha! she thought when Sam took her up on the
idea in a flash, quickly seconded by Molly. There was
no way he could wriggle out of the sessions of treatment now!

'Hello!' called a voice from somewhere at the other
end of the house.

'That's Anna,' said Sam with a smile as she
reached for the diminutive crutches propped against
her chair and slid to the floor. 'She's the 'ceptionist
and it's my job to take the 'pointment book to her
when she comes.'

'I see what you mean about the way she moves on
those things,' Bethan said, amazed by the speed with
which Sam could get about. 'You're going to have to
do some serious practice if she ever decides to challenge you a real race—other than one to get rid of
them.'

'I hope I'm not going to be on them long enough to get proficient,' he said darkly. 'My knee's already much less painful.'

'Well, we'll be able to tell when we get a look at it later on this morning,' Bethan said, fixing him with a stern look. 'In the meantime...'

'In the meantime, I can hear the sound of voices—other than my precocious child—so I'd better get to work.'

He struggled awkwardly out of his chair and across the room, having to stop to work out the logistics of opening the door without getting in the way of it before he disappeared from view.

Bethan followed the sound of his progress as she cradled her mug in her hand then looked up to find Molly's keen gaze fixed on her.

'The little one said you're a doctor,' she said, her voice friendly as she started to stack the breakfast dishes. 'On holiday for a couple of weeks?'

Bethan remembered telling Sam lots of things while she'd been trying to take her mind off her father's injuries.

'That's right. I'm staying at an hotel about half an hour away on the coast.'

Bethan took another sip of coffee but she could feel Molly's eyes on her as she bustled backwards and forwards between the table and the sink.

'What sort of a doctor are you?' she asked after a pause, and Bethan had to hide her smile behind her mug. 'Subtle' and 'Molly' were two words that didn't belong in the same sentence.

'A hospital doctor,' Bethan said innocently, as if she didn't know what the older woman was angling for.

'Then you've done a bit of everything, have you?'

Molly continued hopefully, obviously frustrated that Bethan wasn't being more forthcoming, and Bethan decided to take pity on her.

'Yes, Molly, I've done a bit of everything, but I haven't got the right qualifications to be a GP—not even as a temporary measure to help Josh out.'

'What qualifications would you need?' she demanded, turning with her fists on her hips, soapsuds clinging to them like iridescent bracelets. 'Either you're a doctor or you aren't a doctor, surely?'

'Molly…' Bethan paused while she tried to find a way to explain. 'If you had a sick child who might be going down with meningitis, would you rather take her to someone who's prepared to deal with every different possibility every day or one whose last job was stripping out varicose veins or sorting out piles?'

The older woman subsided onto a chair as her hopeful expression faded.

'Oh, Doctor,' she sighed. 'I knew it seemed too easy, but I did hope I wasn't going to be letting him down.'

'What's going on?' Bethan put her mug down and covered the damp pink hands with her own. 'Is there a problem?'

'It's my sister,' Molly said. 'Dr Josh might have told you I had to go to see her yesterday.'

Bethan nodded. 'He read me your note.'

'She had a fall off the steps in her kitchen, putting her jams away in the cupboard, and broke her arm when she put it out to try to save herself. They put her in plaster and kept her in hospital because she was in shock, but she's coming home tomorrow and she needs someone there to help her—at least in the beginning.'

'How long do you think you'll have to stay with her? Until the cast comes off?'

'Lord love you, no!' exclaimed Molly. 'Just until I can get her organised and she works out how to do things one-handed. I shouldn't be gone more than a week, but that's a week too long for Dr Josh to be without help.'

'And you don't know which way to turn,' Bethan finished, her heart weighted down with the realisation that this was going to be yet another burden on Josh's overladen shoulders.

How on earth was he going to manage to take care of Sam without Molly to keep an eye on her? From what she'd seen this morning, the woman was more of an honorary grandmother than a mere housekeeper.

'Do you see why I was hoping you could help him?' Molly continued doggedly. 'At least he wouldn't have to take the little one with him when he goes out on call at night.'

'He takes her with him?' Bethan said with a frown, disturbed by the idea of a little child being dragged around the county instead of sleeping peacefully in her own bed.

'He'll *have* to if there's no one here to stay with her,' she said simply. 'He wouldn't leave her in the house alone.'

The enormity of Josh's problem came home to her with the force of a battering ram—and he didn't even know about the latest blow yet.

'When do you have to go?' Bethan asked. 'How long has he got to make other arrangements?' Even as she asked the questions she felt herself being dragged into his tangled problems.

'Not till midday tomorrow, but I can't see that he's going to be able to do anything miraculous in the next twenty-four hours when he hasn't managed it in two months.'

'Two months!' Bethan exclaimed. 'I thought his partner had only been gone a few days.'

'Dr Tim has, but Dr Martin's been off sick for two months and he wasn't pulling his weight for a long time before that—ever since his wife was taken ill, in fact.'

Bethan didn't need two guesses to know who had been taking up the slack. If 'Dr Tim' had been in the throes of planning his wedding she could just imagine how many extra shifts Josh had been working.

No wonder he was exhausted…

'If you can think of anything—or anyone—who could help out, even temporarily. Perhaps someone from your hospital might…' Molly shrugged helplessly.

'Can you give me until lunchtime to put my thinking cap on?' Bethan asked as she stood up and carried her mug over to the sink. 'That'll be soon enough to break the bad news to him, anyway. In the meantime, I'm going to wander along and see if there's anything I can do to help out, and if not I can always just watch and see what a GP's job is really like.'

'I'll be keeping my fingers crossed,' Molly said, holding up her hand to demonstrate. 'The practice is in the extension at the end of the corridor. Just follow the sound of voices.'

Bethan walked into a scene of organised chaos when she entered the reception area of the practice.

Sam was sitting on the floor in front of a low table with a colouring book and crayons, chattering away nineteen to the dozen with several other youngsters of various ages.

Every seat in the little room seemed to be taken, and a pretty blonde woman was busily sorting papers and talking on the phone at the same time.

'Hello, Bethan,' Sam called with a smile and a wave, then returned to her colouring with the tip of her tongue caught between her teeth as she concentrated.

The blonde head followed every other one in the room in swivelling towards her.

'So *you're* Sam's Bethan,' the young woman said with a wide friendly smile, offering her hand in welcome. 'I'm Anna. Sam's just been telling us all the story of how you rescued her and her father from their car.'

Bethan felt her cheeks grow warm and knew that she was blushing.

'Anyone would have done the same,' she said with an embarrassed shrug as she moved closer in the vain hope that everyone in the room wouldn't be listening to their conversation. As it was, she was horribly conscious of their eyes on her.

'I was just wondering,' Bethan said diffidently. 'Do you think it would be all right with Josh if I went in the room with him—to observe?'

There was a speculative gleam in the young receptionist's eyes as she looked Bethan over.

'I don't see why not,' she murmured. 'You could slip in when the patient comes out and ask him.'

Anna glanced down at the list in front of her on the desk and snorted softly. 'In fact, he might just welcome you with open arms because the next ones due in are two of the little monsters playing with Sam, and they aren't going to be very happy about having their playtime cut short.'

Bethan grinned and made her way in the direction

Anna pointed out. She wasn't above using adverse circumstances to further her own ends, especially where Dr Joshua Kent was concerned. The man was far too stubborn for his own good.

'Mornin', miss,' said the elderly man on his way out of the treatment room, giving her an old-fashioned salute and completely forgetting that he was holding his prescription in his hand.

'Good morning,' she returned brightly, and stepped into Josh's inner sanctum.

'Bethan. What can I do for you?' he asked in surprise, a slightly harried expression on his face as he glanced towards her then back down at the keyboard. His hair wasn't quite as neat as it had been at breakfast, as if he'd been running his fingers through it, but he hadn't resorted to unbuttoning his collar yet.

'It's more a case of what I can do for you,' she replied as she glanced around, taking in the quiet, clean lines of the furniture and the state-of-the-art computer humming quietly beside him. The vertical blinds at the windows softened the bright sunlight outside and helped to keep the room cool.

'And what's that?'

He leant back in his chair and she saw him gingerly moving his injured leg as if he couldn't find a position to make it comfortable. 'I would have thought you would have been on your way back to your hotel by now, glad to see the last of us.'

'I'll go if you like,' she offered with a mischievous grin when she heard the sound of approaching little feet—boisterously running feet. 'Anna seemed to think you might welcome my presence with your next patients.'

He leant forward to glance at the next name on the

list and threw her a quick grimace just as several sets of small knuckles beat a tattoo on his door.

'Peter *and* Petra? She could be right,' he muttered with a soft groan. 'Will you let them in?'

The next few minutes were chaotic while the three-year-old twins drove their mother to distraction while she tried to nail them down long enough for Josh to examine them, without having to get out of his chair.

'You see, it's still the same, Doctor,' the poor woman said when he'd finished, grabbing tissues from a large box in her bag and helping each of her children in turn to blow their noses. 'It's as if they're all blocked up with a cold the whole time, and it's summertime now. Nothing seems to work. Can't you give them some antibiotics?'

Bethan sighed when she heard the familiar cry, her eyes meeting Josh's over their heads as they exchanged an exasperated look.

So many people still thought that antibiotics were the magic bullet to cure everything. Doctors were on the losing end of the argument if they tried to tell their patients otherwise.

Unfortunately, the end result of over-prescribing and poor patient compliance with completing a course of treatment when it didn't work meant that many bacteria were developing drug-resistant strains.

'Antibiotics wouldn't do any good,' Josh began patiently, and Bethan had the feeling that this wasn't the first time he'd had the same conversation with the young woman. 'The twins aren't suffering from a bacterial infection so giving them antibiotics wouldn't make any difference.'

'But you've got to do *something,* Doctor,' she said, grabbing Peter and a handful of tissues and beginning the process all over again. 'It's driving me mad. All the time their noses are running and their chests are all bunged up. We even got rid of the hamsters because you thought it might be an allergy.'

Bethan was watching the youngsters while their mother made her impassioned appeal. They'd obviously been told that they weren't allowed to touch anything in the doctor's surgery, and once they'd finished scampering around, looking at everything, they wandered across to their mother's capacious handbag and began to rummage inside.

Within seconds they each had a couple of biscuits in each hand and were standing beside her, munching.

A distant bell began to ring in the recesses of Bethan's mind.

Quietly she made her way closer to the two imps and crouched down beside them.

'Are they good?' she whispered with a smile.

'Yeah, but Mummy won't get the choc'late ones 'cos we eat too many,' Peter volunteered.

'How many do you eat?' she asked. 'Lots?'

'Lots and lots,' Petra agreed with a vigorous nod.

'They do, too,' the mother added as she caught the tail end of the conversation. 'It's as if they can't get enough of them. Still, they're wholewheat ones and I know they're getting enough roughage because they never have any difficulty going to the toilet—just the opposite sometimes.'

'Do they have cereal for breakfast?' Bethan asked, then looked across at Josh in horror at her breach of etiquette. 'I'm sorry, Doctor,' she said formally. 'I hope you don't mind, but I just had an idea.'

'Be my guest,' he invited with a wave of his hand, and turned to the puzzled woman. 'Dr...' He paused and glanced back at Bethan and she could see that

he'd suddenly realised that he didn't know her surname.

'Mallory,' she supplied with a wry grin as a terrible
thought flashed through her mind. She'd been to bed
with this man and shared her body with him and he
hadn't even known her full name.

'Dr Mallory is a colleague who works in a hospital
further upcountry,' he continued. 'She's spending a
few weeks on holiday in our area and asked to sit in
with my patients.'

'You'm a glutton for punishment,' the young
woman said bluntly. 'Catch me volunteering to work
on my holiday! What was it you wanted to know?'

'If the twins have cereal for breakfast, and how
much bread and pastry they have during the day.'

'They often have several bowls of cereal—well, the
milk's good for them, isn't it? Middle of the day I
make some sandwiches, then we have the big meal
when their daddy gets home. I usually make a pie or
some pasties because he's hungry at the end of the
day, but I always serve plenty of vegetables with it.
If they get hungry between times I let them help themselves to biscuits.'

Bethan glanced across at Josh and raised an eyebrow, hoping he was picking up on the same clues
and reading the same inferences.

He gave a brief nod and turned back to face his
patients' worried mother.

'Mrs Dark, it's possible that the twins are suffering
from an allergy…'

'But we already got rid of the hamsters and we
don't have any other pets,' she objected.

'This is a different allergy—an allergy to a particular type of food,' he explained calmly. 'It can even
include anything containing that food.'

'But what is it?' she demanded. 'I don't let them have fizzy drinks nor all those snack things with all the E numbers.'

'But they do have a great deal of wheat in their diet,' Bethan pointed out gently. 'It sounds as if they have it at every meal and for all their snacks between meals.'

'But wheat's natural, it's good for you as long as you're not trying to lose weight…isn't it?' demanded the poor woman with a haunted look in her eyes as she gazed from one to the other.

'It's not quite as simple as that,' Josh said gently. 'Look, why don't you pop along to the practice nurse and have a chat about it? She's got some leaflets about planning meals without wheat. If you could stick to it for a couple of weeks we'll be able to tell whether your two imps are responding.'

'But…I've still got to feed my husband, too,' she said in horror. 'How am I going to manage to do two sets of cooking?'

'I think you'll find it's much simpler than that,' Bethan suggested quickly, hoping to strike while the iron was hot. 'Sometimes it can be as easy as changing their cereal to rice instead of wheat, leaving the pastry off their share of the meat filling for the pies and pasties and giving them fruit instead of biscuits during the day.'

The frown on the young woman's forehead lifted and she drew in a deep breath.

'Well, *that* doesn't seem too difficult,' she admitted cautiously. 'I might even put all of us on it to see how it goes. I can always give my husband some extra potatoes—and it will save me having to make pastry!'

She gathered up her bags and her fidgety duo and

went to the door, turning back to look across at Bethan.

'If this sorts these two out I'll be forever grateful,' she said with a smile. 'See you in two weeks.'

'Well done,' Josh murmured as he added a note to the children's files. 'At least you managed to divert her attention from demanding antibiotics, and hopefully you've actually put your finger on the problem. I was almost certain that it was an allergy reaction but, without seeing the little perishers tucking into those biscuits, I had no idea where to start.'

'You sent her along to the practice nurse for information,' Bethan commented while she glowed inside at his praise. 'Does she keep a stock of the various leaflets?'

'Liz also helps me with the pregnant mums, the diabetic clinic and the small group of weight-watchers we've started so she's well up on the various diets.'

He sat back again and massaged his thigh with one hand as though it was aching.

'Who have you got next?' Bethan said with one eye on the clock, concerned that he was in pain and she couldn't do anything about it.

It was still a long time until she could get some ice on his knee, and she would like to bet that he hadn't taken any of the painkillers this morning.

'Mrs Tarrant. Gloria. A nice lady in her mid-forties, if I remember rightly.' He tapped some keys on the computer to bring her file up onto the screen.

'Ah. Yes. The last time I saw her was a year ago for a smear test and before that it was an injection for an exotic foreign holiday.'

There was a hesitant tap on the door and an attractive brunette stuck her head round.

'Oh, I'm sorry, Doctor, I was told you were ready

for me,' she said, seeming terribly flustered. 'Shall I come back in a minute?'

'Come in, Mrs Tarrant, and take a seat,' Josh said, beckoning her in with a smile. 'You're not interrupting anything. This is Dr Mallory, visiting us from civilisation. Now, what can I do for you?'

'Well, I don't know exactly,' she said, glancing nervously from one to the other as she wrung her hands. 'I don't even know whether I'm just wasting your time.'

'Why don't you tell us what it's all about and then we can tell you one way or the other,' he said. 'This way you get two heads for the price of one!'

'All right,' she said quietly, her smile wan, as if whatever was troubling her had been causing her to lose sleep for some time before she'd finally forced herself to come. 'It's... I found... I think I found a lump...in my breast...the right one...not very big, but...' She drew in a gasping breath and glanced apologetically at them again. 'They do tell you to go to your doctor if you find anything, don't they?'

'They certainly do,' Josh said with a smile as he placed his palms down on the desk and tried to stand. 'Ouch!' he muttered as his knee refused to bend and he sat back with a thump.

'Mrs Tarrant, you wouldn't mind if Dr Mallory did the examination, would you? I had a bit of an accident yesterday and I'm supposed to be using those things to get around.' He pointed disgustedly at the hated crutches and Bethan saw a hint of a smile on his patient's mouth.

'I suppose it would be a little difficult for you to balance on one leg while you looked at me,' she agreed, and Bethan was delighted to hear how much stronger her voice was. For some strange reason, the fact that her doctor was on less than perfect form seemed to have reassured her.

'I don't mind at all, provided her hands are cool,' Mrs Tarrant agreed readily. 'It's so warm outside to-day and I've been so nervous that I wouldn't mind if she's been cuddling ice cubes.'

'It could be arranged,' Bethan said with a smile as she directed her across to the examining couch. 'I've arranged a plentiful supply of ice, ready to treat Dr Kent's knee, so I'm sure there'll be some to spare.'

They all grew silent when Mrs Tarrant had removed the clothing from her upper body and lay flat on the bed, Bethan because she was concentrating on the structures she could feel under the woman's skin and the patient because she was still very nervous about what would be found.

'Have you ever had a mammogram?' Bethan asked as she straightened and stepped back from the couch, nodding to indicate that Mrs Tarrant could put her clothes on again.

'Not so far. I don't think the system starts calling women automatically until they reach fifty—at least in Cornwall.'

'That doesn't mean to say that we can't send some-one before that if we think it's necessary,' Josh inter-rupted, his deep voice soothing.

'Good,' Bethan said. 'Because I think it would be a good idea if Mrs Tarrant had an appointment.'

She turned to the waiting woman. 'I'm almost cer-tain that the lump you found is just a little cyst, but unless you have a mammogram I'm *absolutely* certain that you're going to worry yourself to death about it.'

Mrs Tarrant was surprised into a chuckle. 'Am I that easy to read?' she asked.

'You—and every other woman in the country,'

Bethan confided. 'I'd be exactly the same, in spite of the fact that I've got my medical training to fall back on.'

'In that case, I'll send a letter to the hospital,' Josh confirmed. 'In due course you'll be sent an appointment, and as soon as I get the results I'll let you know.'

Mrs Tarrant drew in a deep breath. 'Thank you so much—both of you. You can't know how much happier I'm feeling than when I came in.'

'And there goes another satisfied customer,' Josh quipped. 'The only trouble is it's going to take me at least as long again to do all the paperwork involved in the referral.'

'Tell me about it!' Bethan said. 'Do you remember how much there was of it on a busy night when you did your stint in A and E?'

The rest of the morning went smoothly, apart from the non-appearance of Mrs Pengelly.

Even the elderly cleric who was having urinary problems and needed a prostate examination was good-natured about the fact that it was performed by a woman.

'Women are taking on all sorts of jobs these days—including my own,' he commented once he'd dressed again. 'There are even some scriptures which seem to suggest that God was a woman—not that I believe it for a moment, otherwise why on earth would she have arranged to put the rest of her own kind through so many trials and tribulations to keep the earth populated?'

'I did see a car sticker which said something on the same lines,' Bethan offered with a chuckle. 'It said, "When God created man, She was only joking"!'

The elderly man had been relieved to hear that although rather enlarged his prostate seemed otherwise normal, and when he'd been offered an appointment with the urologist to see if matters could be eased he'd accepted with alacrity...

Unlike Josh, who'd tried to wriggle out of his own appointment in favour of catching up on some of his paperwork.

'No dice,' Bethan said as she plonked the bowl of ice on the end of the couch and stood, waiting. 'Either you climb up here and get it over with or I'll tell all your patients that you're chicken.'

'It's not that I don't want you to do it. It's just that there's so much else to do that—'

'Oh, for heaven's sake, you're wasting more time arguing about it than it would take to do it!' Bethan exclaimed. 'If you're expecting to be able to sit in a car to do your home visits this afternoon, I would have thought you'd welcome the chance to get a bit of movement into your knee.'

'I'll need to do more than sit in a car,' he pointed out as he stumped across and leant back against the couch while he disposed of the crutches. 'I'm going to need to be able to drive the darn thing and climb in and out to get to the patients...that's always sup-posing that the hire company have delivered the thing.'

If Bethan hadn't been watching him she probably wouldn't have noticed the increased colour along his cheekbones as he'd dropped his trousers to give her access to his heavily strapped knee, but it was his words that were more important at that moment.

'If you think you're going to be able to drive with your knee like this, you'd better think again,' she said firmly. 'It's your right knee and you wouldn't even be able to manage an automatic, let alone gallop in and out to see to your patients.'

'It's a case of having no options,' Josh said firmly, his tone strictly no-nonsense. 'I have a list of patients to see this afternoon and I *will* be going out to see them. I have a duty of care towards them as their GP and I will not let them down.'

CHAPTER SEVEN

JOSH was glaring at Bethan as if he was daring her to contradict him, and the space between them was electric, his deep blue eyes almost seeming to shoot sparks at her.

'Of course you'll be seeing them,' Bethan returned calmly. 'The only thing I'm questioning is the way you'll be doing it…and you *won't* be driving.'

'So how *will* I?' he challenged. 'I'm hardly in a fit state to *walk*!'

'I was proposing that I should act as your chauffeur,' she suggested. 'I know I haven't done any GP training so I couldn't do the visits *for* you, but there's nothing to say that I can't go *with* you.'

Josh's leg grew tense in her hand, resisting the work she was trying to do, and she realised that he was gazing up at her as if he were trying to see inside her head—almost as if he was suspecting her of harbouring some hidden agenda.

Gradually she persuaded him to relax his leg, keeping up her ministrations in silence while he worked through his troubling thoughts.

Finally, he seemed to come to a decision.

'I suppose it makes sense,' he conceded. 'Apart from any other considerations, you'd probably never *find* half of the patients. Some addresses just consist of the name of a farm and the nearest village—no numbers or street names at all!'

Once he'd relaxed enough she began taking his knee through a series of passive exercises, watching the involuntary tightening of the muscles at the corners of his mouth to know when she'd taken it far enough. She knew already that he wasn't someone to complain about pain, but something inside her rebelled at the idea of putting him through any more than absolutely necessary.

'Now for the good part,' she said with an evil grin, and wrapped his knee in a layer of ice.

The cold drew an agonised groan out of him as it made contact, even though she'd surrounded it with a layer of cloth, but soon his skin grew accustomed to it and he sighed as it started to help to ease the pain.

'Bearable?' she questioned, shocked to discover that her hands had clenched into tight fists at the idea that she was hurting him.

'I'll live,' he agreed wryly. 'I'm just glad you weren't still angry with me when it was time to put the ice on. I think you're a closet sadist.'

'Perhaps you'd better remember that if you want to argue with me,' she teased lightly, and returned to business. 'It doesn't need to stay on for very long at a time, then it can go back into the freezer ready for next time. As soon as Anna buzzes to let you know your next patient has arrived I'll replace it with a slightly lighter dressing.'

The rest of the session passed relatively easily as they found ways of working together which eased the load on Josh's leg.

He was still strangely wary of her and she was conscious at intervals that his dark blue eyes were watching her, almost as if he wanted to dissect her motives for being there.

Molly had lunch ready and waiting by the time the

morning's patients were finished, and Sam was bursting with things to tell them about her busy morning.

'I been helping to make lots of food to put in the freezer,' she announced importantly. 'Then we took all the sheets off Daddy's and my beds and put them in the washing machine and I helped to put the clean ones on. And s'afternoon, Molly 'n' me are going to make some cakes.'

At the mention of Josh's bed Bethan's heart gave an extra thump and her eyes widened as they flew across to meet his. For a brief moment the deep blue almost seemed to sear into her and she knew that he was remembering the same scenes which were playing through her mind.

As she watched, the shutters came down and he dragged his gaze away, turning to focus on his daughter for the rest of the meal and leaving Bethan feeling strangely lonely.

Then it was time for an afternoon of home visits.

'The back of the car is full,' Bethan exclaimed when she followed him out into the yard to see a new vehicle standing ready.

'It's the stuff from my own car,' Josh said as he automatically started to manoeuvre himself around to the driver's door on his crutches. 'My insurance company arranged for all my kit to be collected from the locked compound at the garage where it was towed and piled it into this one. It's a good job they did—I was obviously too far out of it to remember that there were all sorts of drugs in there, not to mention my prescription pad.'

Bethan could have kicked herself for not thinking about it at the time too. It would have been so easy for her to have loaded at least his bag into the ambulance with him. But working exclusively in a hospital, as she did, she'd never had to think about the fact that a GP had a bag to keep an eye on.

'Have you bought the car?' she asked as she wordlessly took him by the elbow and directed him round to the passenger side instead.

'It's on loan until the insurance claim's been sorted out, but it *is* available for purchase if I like it.'

'Well, I'll be sure to tell you what I think of the handling,' she said cheekily as she turned the key in the ignition.

'It's got more leg room than your Midgetmobile,' he fired back, and when she just laughed he started giving her the directions to their first destination.

Their visits were a completely mixed bunch and Josh occupied the travelling time between each onc by giving her a potted history of the patient they were about to see.

The first was a diabetic woman who had just returned home after her second leg had been amputated.

'She shouldn't have lost *either* leg,' Josh said angrily. 'It's a blatant case of self-neglect despite everything we've tried to do. She resents the fact that she's become diabetic so she's decided to kill herself by inches—and stones—and is crucifying her family in the process.'

'Has she seen a psychologist?' Bethan asked when they were on their way to their second visit, her spirits utterly dampened by the gargantuan woman's bitter tongue.

'She utterly refuses, in spite of the fact that her husband begged her to. Poor man still loves her and can't bear to see what she's doing to herself.'

Their next visit was to a young woman with three young children in the early stages of a chicken-pox infection.

'Not a good idea to have this lot brought into a crowded waiting room,' Josh said when they were greeted at the gate by three very spotty children.

'They've been absolutely miserable in this hot weather,' their mother said, looking quite exhausted. 'I thought it was chicken pox when I saw the tops of the spots, and gave them each a bottle of calamine lotion and some cotton wool balls to apply it to each other. They've looked like Coco the clown ever since breakfast.'

'I suppose the only consolation is that you've got it all over at once,' Bethan pointed out. 'At least this is one of the childish illnesses you won't have to deal with again.'

'There are still several more to go so I still might end up going mad,' the young woman said darkly, but they could tell that underneath the grumbling she loved her children dearly and was coping very well.

As they settled themselves in the car Bethan suggested that they might call in at her hotel at some stage so that she could have a quick change of clothes.

At the back of her mind was the possibility that Josh might suggest that she stayed on at his house to help him out—at least until his knee had recovered enough so that he could drive.

She knew that he'd found her presence helpful today because he'd finally admitted it, but whether he would want her to stay on—or would even be needing her to stay on if he managed to find a qualified locum—was another matter.

The idea she wouldn't allow herself to explore was the possibility that he might have found their lovemaking as spectacular as she had, even though it had been her first time, and would want to explore the more intimate side of their relationship too.

'The next one is Mrs Pengelly who phoned the practice this morning, wanting me to come out straight away,' Josh said, breaking into Bethan's heated musings, and she had to force herself to concentrate on the information he was giving her.

'She's the one who didn't bother to turn up for the ten-thirty appointment?'

'That's right. She's a rather demanding patient at the best of times, and this time she said she was having problems with her legs. Apparently they hurt so badly that she could hardly get out of bed to come to the phone.'

'So now you're worried that after all those times of crying wolf this time she's really ill?'

'Exactly. Anna tried to phone her when she didn't show up but there was no answer.'

Bethan pulled up outside a small, neat bungalow, one of several fairly new ones built on the edge of a typically picturesque little Cornish village.

While Josh was extricating himself from the car Bethan let herself into the front garden and went to ring the bell.

'Is that you, Dr Kent?' called an inquisitive voice from the garden next door, and a head of silvery white curls surrounding the weather-beaten face of an elderly pixie peered over a neatly clipped hedge.

'Hello, Mrs Penno. You're looking well,' Josh said with a smile.

'Haven't felt so good in years, Doctor,' she said with an emphatic nod. 'You were quite right about that hip of mine. That operation has made life worth living again. Mind you, that physiotherapist afterwards was a real slave driver, but it was all worth it in the end.'

'I couldn't be more pleased for you,' he said. 'I suppose you're back to organising the village again.'

'Oh, I've slowed up a bit these days, now that I'm getting on a bit,' she confided. 'I haven't got the farm any more but I still do the flowers and the cleaning rota for the church and organise the hanging baskets and the planting round the green for our entry for the best-kept village. Then, of course, there's the Women's Institute and fund-raising for Cancer Research and the Red Cross.'

'Mrs Penno, you put the rest of us to shame,' Josh said with a laugh.

'You make me feel exhausted, just listening to you,' Bethan agreed.

'You weren't looking for Mrs Pengelly, were you?' Mrs Penno asked, tilting her head to one side like an inquisitive little bird. 'Her friend called around about nine o'clock this morning and they walked into the village to catch the bus into Truro.'

'Do you know when she'll be home?' Josh asked.

Out of the corner of her eye Bethan saw the muscles on his arms tighten into hawsers as he clenched his hands tightly around his crutches, but she realised from the pleasant way he spoke that Mrs Penno would never know that he was seething.

'Well, on her way out, she did say that the two of them were going to have a lovely day together, browsing through the shops. They asked me if I wanted to go with them but I'd rather be pottering in my garden on a day like this, doing a bit of dead-heading.'

'I see,' he said quietly as he turned back towards the car.

'Did you want me to give her a message, Doctor? It's no bother.'

'Oh, just tell her I called round,' he said mildly, and set off down the path.

'Wretched woman,' he snarled as he shoved his bag away by his feet and tightened the seat belt across his body with a vicious jerk. 'Wasting my time trailing all the way out here because her legs hurt her too badly to manage to come into the surgery. They certainly got better in a hurry when her friend came calling. It's enough to make you feel like insisting that she comes in to the surgery for her appointments for ever more.'

'Except the *next* time she might *really* be ill and you'd never forgive yourself if she was lying here in a coma when you could have prevented it.'

Bethan shot a glance at him and grinned. 'You try to look like the big bad wolf with your frown and your serious expressions, but you're soft as butter—and they all know it.'

He was startled into a chuckle.

'And I thought I'd managed to keep it a closely guarded secret,' he mourned.

'Ha!' Bethan mocked. '"Please Daddy, just one more go on the twisty tower thing"!' she mimicked, letting him know she hadn't forgotten the first time she'd seen him with Sam. 'I'll have you know that I had your measure the first time I saw you!'

She could only snatch brief glimpses of him as she concentrated on driving the strange car through the meandering lanes, but suddenly she realised that his eyes were sparkling again and the creases beside his eyes were from humour rather than strain.

'It's not nice to gloat,' he complained, but failed utterly to sound hurt.

'Ah, but who said I was nice?' she challenged as

they drew up outside the tiny cottage where his next patient lived.

'Mr Yandall lives here—has done since the day he was born. Unfortunately, he's been suffering from increasingly severe angina for the past four years or so, and he can't keep up with his garden any more. He's been waiting for heart surgery and I've finally found out that he's on the short-list.'

Josh opened the door of Mr Yandall's cottage without bothering to knock, simply calling out to let the old man know who it was.

'Come you in, boy. Kettle's on,' a voice called back, and Josh opened the door fully.

He led the way into the single downstairs room just as the elderly man straightened out of his chair.

'Ah, you've brought comp'ny this time. Pretty maid, too,' he said with a wicked twinkle in his faded blue eyes as he held out a welcoming hand, then sat straight back down again as soon as he'd greeted both of them. 'Did she give you the bruises when you stepped out of line?'

'What makes you think that?' Bethan asked with a grin, liking the outspoken old man immediately. 'Does he often step out of line?'

The other patients had all expressed horror at Josh's all too visible injuries, but Mr Yandall was the first one to have teased him about them.

'Never been known to, more's the pity,' the old man said with a theatrically mournful air. 'Not my idea of what bein' young's about. Time enough when you get to my age to start behavin' yourself, just in case God's got his eye on you.'

'Well, this time it was just an argument between a car and a hedge,' Josh told him. 'Bethan was the guardian angel who came along and took care of Sam and me.'

'And how's the little maid? How're her legs? Did the operation do the job?' Mr Yandall asked, as concerned as if Sam was a close relative.

'It looks like it, but we're still keeping our fingers crossed.'

'Well, you tell the little maid that there's some apples waiting for 'er to pick soon as she's ready. You bring 'er here soon as she's allowed on rough ground.'

'I will, Mr Yandall, and that's a promise.'

While they'd been talking Josh had made a pot of tea and poured three cups, as though the whole thing was second nature. He even knew where the biscuit tin was kept.

'Well, then, boy,' the old man said eagerly when they were all sitting with their cups. 'Have you got any news for me? I hope so or that's a waste of a good chocolate biscuit.'

'At long last, yes, Mr Yandall,' Josh confirmed with a chuckle. 'Your name's gone up on the list to be operated on in the new cardiac unit. You won't have to face travelling all the way up to London.'

''Bout time they got that running, too,' Mr Yandall fired back. 'Disgraceful the way anyone west of Bristol couldn't get operated on without they go to London. 'Tis the same every time. Too many chiefs up there and not enough Indians anywhere else.'

'Don't tell *me*—you're preaching to the converted,' Josh said, raising one hand in surrender. 'You tell my pretty friend. She's a doctor upcountry, and I'm sure if you work your charms on her you could get her to move down here where she'd be more appreciated.'

'Go on with you,' the old man chided with a rusty

chuckle. 'You're the young buck with the good looks—*you* persuade her. You can use more than words.'

Josh laughed at his innuendo but Bethan could see that his teasing had left the younger man looking distinctly uncomfortable, as if he'd reminded Josh of something he'd rather forget.

Soon after that Josh stopped his socialising long enough to check the old man over and make certain that he had enough tablets close at hand in case of an angina attack.

'Don't you worry, boy,' he growled. 'Now I know the operation is getting closer I won't forget my dynamite. I've got to make sure the ticker keeps going long enough that they can mend it.'

Once they were back on the road Bethan said how much she'd enjoyed talking to the old man, but Josh hardly did more than grunt in reply before he lapsed into an uneasy silence.

Bethan was just gathering up the courage to ask him what was wrong when he spoke.

'I've been thinking about what you said, Bethan,' he began slowly, and she was conscious that he'd turned slightly so that he was able to watch her while he spoke.

'Just as we arrived at Mr Yandall's you said jokingly that perhaps you weren't nice. It's not true because you are...in fact, you're a very nice person. Someone who would willingly put herself in danger to try to protect a stranger's child from a runaway bull and then, just hours later, dangles upside down over a car full of petrol vapour to help the stupid driver who nearly killed himself and his daughter because he was falling asleep at the wheel.'

'You're not—' Bethan began.

She didn't get any further because Josh simply drew another breath and continued.

'And, as if that wasn't enough, you babysat Sam for hours at the hospital, played taxi-driver and then babysat both of us for the night. Now, you tell me which one of us is soft as butter?'

Bethan was feeling distinctly uncomfortable and her cheeks were blazing by the time he finished, and all she could think of doing to lighten the atmosphere was try to make a joke.

'I've never heard it called babysitting before,' she murmured as she thought about their time together last night.

This time the silence between them went on for a long time and Bethan didn't dare look at him, silently cursing her unruly tongue. Why couldn't she have graciously accepted his compliments and left it at that? Her suggestive remark had obviously given him the wrong idea about her and now he was—

'I would have said I was far too old to need a baby-sitter, but after last night... Oh, Bethan, I owe you an apology.'

'An apology?' she echoed as her stomach clenched in dismay. How could she bear it if he ruined the most magical event of her life?

'Yes,' he said grimly, and sighed. 'You've done so much for Sam and me—are *still* doing so much, in spite of the fact that you're supposed to be on holiday. All day I've been feeling so guilty about the way I took advantage of you when you were only trying to help, and then, to make matters worse, I went and fell asleep!'

Bethan couldn't help the nervous giggle that escaped her. Her brain was whirling with everything he'd just said but it was that last phrase and the disgust in his tone that lingered.

'Well, you *had* taken some painkillers and you *were* exhausted,' she offered in mitigation, knowing what a fragile flower the male ego could be.

'But that still isn't any excuse for taking advantage of you,' he insisted.

'Look, it's not such a—'

'No, Bethan, let me finish,' Josh interrupted firmly. 'You were saying only a little while ago that you wanted to pick up a change of clothing. I take it that means that you're thinking about volunteering to stay at Pendruccombe a bit longer?'

'Well, yes, I was,' she agreed tentatively, then rushed into a hasty justification. 'It's obvious that you're temporarily stuck and I thought it would give you the breathing space you needed to organise something more permanent.'

She knew she was babbling, but just the thought that he might be glad to see her gone was making her heart hammer. Did he think she was being too presumptuous and pushing in where she wasn't needed? *Was* he going to tell her that he'd rather she didn't stay on any longer?

'I have to admit that, with the best will in the world, I couldn't have coped today without your help,' he began briskly, and suddenly she found herself stupidly close to tears.

'You've got a good manner with the patients and good instincts for what might be hidden underneath what they're telling you,' he continued, apparently oblivious of the way her hands were trembling with relief. 'But that doesn't mean we can escape from the fact that before you came down to Cornwall for your holiday you hadn't even *thought* about applying for

GP training, and I'm not registered with the General Medical Council as a trainer.

'Having said that, even if you *have* done the right specialities during your training, and you *were* to get permission to help out on a limited basis, we would have to lay down some ground rules.'

'Such as?' Bethan prompted shakily, prepared to agree to almost anything as her spirits started to rise inside her like helium-filled balloons on a hot day.

It really sounded as if he was saying that he was going to approach the GMC for permission for her to stay and help him out. It sounded as if, far from wanting to get rid of her, he actually wanted her to stay on.

'Well, first of all, you'd have to understand that my patients are ultimately my responsibility and, as such, I would have to sit in with you while you saw them.'

'That's perfectly reasonable, and no different from what happened today,' she pointed out. 'Obviously, with your knee so painful, some things *are* going to be difficult for you.'

'The problem arises when we get to night-time,' he said with a frown. 'I can hardly rely on calling a taxi out and it wouldn't be fair to drag you out of bed every time the phone rang to drive me all over the county.'

'I know you said you're having difficulty finding a locum, but how did you manage yesterday?' she asked, suddenly realising that the phone hadn't started ringing until this morning. 'As far as I know, you weren't called out once—or did you have someone covering for you?'

'A doctor in a neighbouring village—Laurence Foster—was covering. He's been retired for several years now, but is willing to cover me for the odd night when things go mad.'

'Then, as long as the GMC approve, I don't see that we've got a problem,' she said with a smile, hoping she didn't look as giddy as she felt.

'There's just one more thing,' he said quietly. 'You have my promise that there wouldn't be any repeat of...of what happened last night. In spite of the fact that you'd be living in my house, you wouldn't have to worry that I was going to take advantage of the situation. The relationship between us would be strictly professional.'

'And?' she forced herself to ask matter-of-factly, while the helium balloons inside her began to sink back to earth.

For the first time in her life she'd found a man who lit fires in her soul and here he was systematically trying to put them out. Was there no justice in the world?

'And I promise that in the time you were helping out I'd be moving heaven and earth to try to find a properly qualified locum so that I didn't completely ruin your holiday.'

Bethan was silent while she came to terms with her disappointment. If she'd spoken at that moment, she had a horrible feeling that she would have howled with frustration.

'Well?' he prompted, and the only consolation she had was that he seemed totally unaware that his hands were clenched into knots on his thighs. Perhaps he wasn't quite as calm and dispassionate about the whole situation as he wanted her to think.

'You said you want our relationship to be professional?' she questioned bleakly.

'I think that would be best,' Josh agreed.

'Does that mean that you'd rather I didn't have anything to do with Sam?' Her heart ached at the thought that she might have to keep her distance from the delightful child—not that she could see how it would be possible with Molly going away and Josh on crutches.

'That's up to you,' he said, his tone utterly neutral, but she saw the way his knuckles whitened as he clenched them again and knew that the question had touched something inside him.

'I try to keep her out of the practice as much as possible,' he continued. 'But she's known most of the staff for a couple of years now and thinks of them as her extended family. If you'd rather not see her I could always ask Molly to—'

'That's not what I meant at all!' Bethan shot back at him, horrified that he could have misunderstood so badly. 'I think she's a wonderful little girl and I thoroughly enjoyed taking care of her yesterday.'

'Then what…?'

'What I meant was that if this entirely professional relationship meant that you were expecting me to keep my distance from her then I was going to find it very difficult. I can't tell you how much I admire her spirit. She's an absolute credit to you and I can't see her being a bother at all.'

A dreadful thought suddenly struck her.

'Josh… Molly did have a chance to talk to you about her sister, didn't she?' she demanded urgently.

'Her sister? What about?' He sounded so puzzled that for a moment she wondered if he'd remembered that he'd found the note on the kitchen table.

'Oh, yes, I remember now. That's where Molly had gone yesterday when we got home. What's the matter? Did she say anything to you?'

Bethan groaned. 'I knew there was something she was going to tell you but, with Sam chattering over lunch, it completely went out of my mind.'

'Is there a problem? What was the matter with her?'

'Yes, I'm afraid there *is* a problem,' she said grimly. 'She'd had a fall and has broken her arm, and when they let her out of hospital tomorrow she's going to need Molly with her for a few days to help her set things up for one-handed living until the cast can come off.'

'Damn, damn, damn,' Josh muttered through gritted teeth as he dropped his head back against the headrest.

This time Bethan didn't feel like teasing him with her grandmother's litany. She'd known when she'd first heard about it that this was going to be just one more blow on top of a series of blows, but she hadn't realised then just how much his misfortune would affect her.

'She hopes it's only going to be for a few days and she's been spending today going through the house like a dose of salts and filling the freezer up with meals so that you won't starve.'

'Is *that* why she's been in a cooking frenzy today?' he demanded. 'I was beginning to worry that she'd heard there was going to be a second flood the way she was carrying on.'

Out of the corner of her eye she saw the tired smile lighten his expression.

'Sam's had the time of her life today as acting cook's assistant,' Bethan said. 'You'll probably get an ounce by ounce replay of how each dish was made as you eat it.'

'Well, they say misery loves company—you'll be listening, too!'

'But there will be compensations,' Bethan pointed

out quietly as a warm glow began to fill her at the thought that she was going to be staying on at Pendruccombe. If he managed to get permission, she would actually be working by his side for several more days and would be sharing those meals with him.

'Compensations?' he asked, his tone almost wary.

'Well, for a start, if I'm busy I won't be wandering around the countryside frightening the sheep when I try to hold conversations with them.'

'You...what?'

'Well, I couldn't find anyone else to talk to,' she explained with a shrug.

'What on earth made you come to Cornwall, then? Wasn't there someone you could have shared the holiday with?'

Suddenly her stomach sank as if it had just gone down in a high-speed lift. Simon. She'd completely forgotten about Simon.

Just a few days ago she'd believed her heart had been irretrievably broken when she'd discovered that he was planning to go away with another woman, but now when she tried to remember what he looked like it was almost as if she was trying to see him from a great distance.

'No,' she murmured, realising that Josh was waiting for an answer. 'There was no one to share the holiday with. In fact, one of the reasons I chose Cornwall was because I was hoping to have the time to decide what direction I wanted to go with my career...with my life...'

CHAPTER EIGHT

BETHAN saw the hotel just up ahead and indicated that she was going to turn, glad that there wasn't time for Josh to ask her what she'd meant.

With any luck, by the time she'd collected her clothes he'd have forgotten what they'd been talking about and the subject would be dropped. The last thing she wanted to talk about was her chaotic state of mind—her lost dreams and her niggling dissatisfaction with her professional life.

It only took her ten minutes to change into a pair of lightweight linen trousers and a sleeveless blouse and pack everything else up into her two small suitcases, then she stood just inside the doorway and glanced around one last time to see if she'd forgotten anything.

She'd booked for the first two weeks in August and had already paid for the room for the full fortnight so could return at any time if Josh managed to find the locum he needed, but secretly she was hoping that nothing would happen to cut her time short with him. Nice as it was, she hoped she wasn't going to be seeing this room again.

She gave a short laugh and the sound echoed round the empty room.

'What a fool,' she whispered as she caught sight of herself in the rather ornate mirror over the dressing-table on the other side of the room.

At first glance she looked no different, the same person wearing the same clothes with the same short dark hair and dark eyes…but it was the expression in those eyes which had changed.

'There you are, old enough and intelligent enough to know better and you've gone and fallen in love with the man in the space of a day!'

Less than that, really, she corrected herself when she remembered the way she'd welcomed his love-making.

'Oh, Gran, you must be shaking your head at me,' she murmured as she opened the door and bent down to grasp the suitcase handles. 'This isn't at all the way you brought me up, but…'

The lift was already waiting for her at her floor and she stepped inside. Smoky mirrors surrounded the small cubicle and she couldn't avoid looking at herself again.

This close she could see the way her dark eyes were gleaming with a secret excitement and the way the pulse at the base of her throat was racing with the thought that Josh was waiting for her downstairs.

'But you know what, Gran?' she murmured aloud in the cocooned seclusion, her chin tilting up just a notch. 'I don't care… I don't care what anyone thinks any more. This…whatever is happening between Josh and me…it feels right. More right than anything else in my life.'

The muted 'ping' warned her that she'd arrived on the ground floor and the doors slid open.

The first thing she saw was Josh, leaning against one of the pillars in the hotel's reception area, his dark hair slightly tousled and the muscles on his forearms taut under his rolled-up sleeves as he balanced on his crutches.

Bethan's heart bounded with a series of extra beats

and desire spiralled deep inside her as a smile crept over her face.

'I decided I might just as well bring the lot with me,' she said brightly when he caught sight of her and turned to walk beside her to the front door. 'It will save me having to come back again for more clothing if it takes longer than you hope to get things sorted out. The room's paid for until the end of my holiday so I can always return here at any time if you don't need me any more.'

'You're mad, you know,' Josh said with a shake of his head as they set off on the return journey towards Pendruccombe. 'You've paid for two weeks of relative luxury in that rather swish hotel. It's got a gym and a pool and it's set in the middle of beautiful scenery with a sandy beach only a short walk away, and you're cheerfully giving it up for what, in effect, is a working holiday. If you were going to change places with another doctor you could at least have chosen somewhere like St Lucia or...'

'What do you mean?' Bethan asked, as if scandalised. 'Haven't you heard that Cornwall's been having better weather than large chunks of mainland Europe this summer? You're living in a top holiday hotspot so don't knock it.'

'Pendruccombe is hardly likely to be on anyone's list of preferred summer resorts,' he scoffed with a wry grin. 'The nearest we come to a beach or even a swimming pool at this time of year is that little trickle of water running through the ford.'

'True, but you must admit that you do have almost everything else holidaymakers could possibly want, and all of it within easy reach,' she pointed out.

'There's hiking, trekking and rock-climbing on the moors, as well as canoeing, wind-surfing and sailing on the reservoirs if you don't want to make the journey to visit a section of the longest stretch of unbroken coastline of any county in England... And that's without mentioning all the historic buildings and theme parks and fascinating towns and villages and—'

'All right, all right,' Josh conceded with an answering laugh. 'I agree that Cornwall's got everything, but all you've done is prove to me that you *are* mad—who would want to swap all that for days of hard work and nights of no sleep?'

'Perhaps someone who prefers to keep busy during the day so that she can appreciate the sleep she *does* get at night,' she replied candidly. 'I wasn't brought up to expect a free ride through life.'

'You certainly won't get that, working in A and E,' he agreed. 'Was that why you chose it as a speciality?'

'I don't know that I *did* choose it,' she said thoughtfully. 'That's one of the things I was supposed to be thinking about on this holiday.'

'What other options are open to you?' he asked and, from his tone and the way he'd angled his body so that he could watch her, she realised that he wasn't just making conversation. He seemed to be genuinely interested in her reply.

'At first, I did think of specialising in paediatric intensive care, but after three months I realised it wasn't right for me. I love children but I nearly broke my heart every time we lost one, no matter how badly disabled they would have been if they'd survived. I finished that six-month stint in straight paediatrics.'

'I told you...soft as butter,' he murmured tauntingly, and when she caught a glimpse of the laughter in his eyes she had to laugh too, revelling in the close, companionable feeling she felt flowing between them.

'Since then?' he prompted when she didn't continue immediately.

'I did a spell in geriatrics after that—'

'From one extreme to the other,' he broke in with a chuckle. 'You're obviously a glutton for punishment, like Mrs Dark said.'

'Then...' Bethan continued forcefully, deliberately ignoring his teasing, 'I did six months of medical and then six months of obstetrics and gynaecology, before ending up in A and E.'

'And which did you prefer?'

'That's just the problem,' she said with a grimace. 'I actually enjoyed them all for different reasons. I suppose that's why I'm having such a problem, making the decision. So far A and E seems to come closest to ideal, with plenty of variety and plenty of hands-on contact with the patients...'

Except for the fact that Simon has applied for the consultancy in that same A and E department, a little voice inside her head reminded her, jolting her out of her happy mood.

'I hate to tell you this,' Josh said, with laughter lingering in his voice, neatly cutting off her uncomfortable thoughts. 'I'm not up on all the latest regulations, but it sounds to me as if you've amassed a viable set of credentials to apply for a position as a GP registrar. If you're not very careful you could end up being one of us—the faceless, unsung heroes of the NHS.'

Before she had a chance to comment on the idea the car was filled with the warbling sound of his mobile phone.

'Hello?' he rapped tersely, and Bethan strained her

ears to try to hear what the voice on the other end was saying.

'When?' he demanded. 'How bad is he?' There was another pause, filled with tantalising half-words. 'When's the air ambulance due? Do they want me there?'

Less than a minute later he smacked the receiver down with a heartfelt, 'Damn.'

'What's the matter?' Bethan asked, flicking worried glances at his set expression.

'It's Mr Yandall. Apparently he went for a walk in his garden to look at his apple trees and his phone rang. You saw how steep his garden is, but the silly man tried to hurry back to the house in time to answer it and collapsed. When his grandson couldn't get a reply he phoned a neighbour who went to look for him and rang for the emergency services.'

'Is he all right?' Bethan asked, feeling quite sick when she realised that it must have happened not long after they'd left him.

'Anna said the paramedics have called the air ambulance out to pick him up so he can be taken directly to hospital for assessment. The paramedic's already got him on oxygen and they've been in contact with the hospital specialist to make sure they've given him all the right medication.'

'So it's just wait and see,' she concluded, feeling horribly powerless. At least in her own A and E department she would be able to stick her head around a door or pick up an internal phone to ask for an update on a patient...

The rest of the journey was completed in silence, each of them wrapped up in their separate thoughts.

A quick glance at Josh's face told Bethan that he was regretting being too far away to have taken care of Mr Yandall himself. She'd seen what a good rapport he'd had with the elderly man and couldn't help crossing her fingers that he would survive this setback.

Josh was very preoccupied for the rest of the afternoon, shutting himself away in his treatment room with a pile of paperwork.

He appeared when it was time for their meal, rousing himself enough to listen to Sam while she chattered over her supper and reading to her when she'd been tucked into bed.

He submitted silently to another session of mobilisation of his knee and barely winced when she applied the ice, his thoughts obviously turned inward as if he was struggling with a problem.

She'd been pleased to see that most of the swelling had gone down but realised that he really wasn't in the mood to talk about the improvement.

Several times during the wildlife programme she'd switched on she felt as if he was watching her, but she refused to look. If he had something on his mind all he had to do was open his mouth and speak.

Finally, after an entire evening of monosyllabic answers, Bethan couldn't stand it any longer and turned on him.

'For heaven's sake, don't just sit there, glowering at me,' she snapped. 'If I've done something wrong, tell me!'

'I'm not glowering...I'm just thinking,' he said with a frown. 'And you haven't done anything wrong.'

'Then you're brooding about Mr Yandall,' she said in exasperation. 'You're his GP. Why don't you phone up the hospital and find out how he is? Better still, tell me where to find the number and I'll dial it for you.'

Josh didn't even need to look the number up. It was engraved on his memory after several years in practice in the area.

It only took a couple of minutes for him to be put in contact with someone who knew what had happened to Mr Yandall on admission.

There were several minutes of hearing Josh say 'Hmm' and 'Uh-huh' in a typical 'doctorly' way which nearly drove her mad before he put the phone down.

'Well?' she demanded, knowing from his changed expression that things weren't as bad as he'd feared. 'How is he?'

'They've got him stabilised but the surgeon's decided that as he's already in and tested to within an inch of his life they're going to keep him in and do his surgery as soon as there's a big enough gap on the list.'

'Talk about an ill wind,' Bethan laughed, quite giddy with relief. 'I know he came pretty close to dying today—'

'Through his own pig-headedness,' Josh cut in. 'He knew damn well his garden's far too steep for him to manage in his condition, and then to try to hurry—uphill—to get to the phone. He was just asking for trouble!'

'And, instead of a very final leap closer to heaven, he's ended up getting a large leap closer to having his heart surgery,' she finished in delight, so glad that the story looked as if it was going to have a happy ending.

Silence fell briefly again while Bethan mulled over the day's events. It was lovely to have everything end on a positive note but it still felt strange…

'I was just thinking how different this is from working in a hospital,' she said aloud. 'There, we either see patients who have already been diagnosed by their GPs as needing treatment for a particular condition or they've been sent in for further investigation to make a diagnosis. A and E is a special case because it's more like crisis management—or it should be if people used their GPs properly—but in almost every case we see a patient just for one particular incident or crisis or operation…whatever.'

'And?' he prompted, lounging back into the corner of the settee with both legs sprawled across the cushions, his intent gaze showing his keen interest in spite of his relaxed posture.

'Well, it's just so different in general practice,' Bethan explained, her ideas coming in fits and starts as she tried to put her thoughts into words. 'Before Laurence decided to retire he'd presumably worked in the same area for most of his life. He's probably seen several generations of children born to some families—seen them as newborns and ended up as GP to their children as well.'

She paused a moment to gather her thoughts, appreciating the way he gave her time, without interrupting.

'It seems to me that when a patient suffers from a particular disease process, such as diabetes or asthma, a GP is closely involved in planning a strategy for the management of that disease for the rest of the patient's life. That's the sort of continuity patients don't get in hospital.'

There was a smile in Josh's dark blue eyes as he waited for her to draw the threads she'd woven into a conclusion.

'I suppose… In the end, I suppose it all comes

down to a series of old-fashioned words such as involvement, responsibility and commitment, not just to your work and your patients, because all doctors should have that, but as a GP it also includes the whole community.'

'That's when you also start to include words such as belonging and interdependence and trust,' he said softly, finally making her monologue a dialogue, a strange expression stealing across his face as he watched her. 'And the more you think about it the bigger and more important it gets. And sometimes,' he added, so softly it was almost as if he was talking to himself, 'sometimes you need a comparative outsider to remind you why you thought the job was worthwhile in the first place.'

Her alarm hadn't even gone off the next morning when Bethan heard the rhythmic thump of Josh's crutches along the landing.

She was just thinking that he was up earlier than usual when she suddenly realised that they were going the wrong way—not towards the bathroom but coming closer to her door.

'Bethan,' she heard him call softly as his fingers tapped out a tattoo on the panelled door. 'Are you awake?'

She groaned. It didn't feel as if she'd been to sleep!

The phone seemed to have been ringing all night, starting with the farmer's wife with breathing difficulties and chest pain just after midnight. In the end, when she hadn't responded very well to medication, Josh had decided to call the ambulance out to transfer her to hospital for further tests in the morning.

They'd barely arrived back inside the door when another patient had rung, in agony from acute abdominal pain. Josh had already known that he was a diverticulitis sufferer and that pain medication would probably be all that was needed, but it had still meant a journey of nearly half an hour each way to the furthest edge of his catchment area to administer it.

They'd actually had time to fall asleep before the phone had rung again at four and they'd been on their way in a hurry to an acute asthma attack, taking with them the portable nebuliser.

Now it was—she cracked one eye open round the edge of the duvet to peer at her alarm clock and groaned again—not even six o'clock and he was up again, and she hadn't even heard the phone ring this time.

'Bethan!' he called again, obviously trying not to wake Molly and Sam.

'OK! Coming!' she called back while she steeled herself to roll over and throw the covers back.

No wonder he'd been ready to fall asleep behind the wheel if this was the sort of pace he'd been trying to maintain while his colleagues were away.

She stretched her feet out from under the duvet and her nightdress had slid all the way up to the top of her thighs just as her door swung open.

'Josh!' she squeaked indignantly, and grabbed the hem with both hands to drag it down towards her knees. 'What are you doing in here?'

'You told me to come in,' he said, leaning against the doorframe while his dark blue eyes outlined the slender shape of her legs. The intensity of his gaze was almost as potent as a caress as she curled them up and tucked her feet back under the covers.

'I said I was coming,' she corrected him, her eyes helplessly drawn to the gaping crossover of his dark blue towelling robe and the way it revealed the silky whorls of hair on his chest before she managed to drag them away. 'I...I didn't even hear the phone ring or I'd be dressed by now. What is it this time? How far have we got to go?'

'Actually, it's not another patient,' he said softly. 'I wanted to have a word with you while everything was quiet.'

'Oh? What about?' She slid up a bit and propped a pillow behind her back before she gestured towards the end of her bed. 'You might as well make yourself comfortable while you can.'

Josh shouldered himself away from the doorway and hobbled across the room, letting the door swing shut behind him. He sighed gratefully as he sank onto the end of the bed and laid his crutches on the floor, before stretching his leg out.

Suddenly Bethan was almost suffocatingly aware of how small the room had become once he'd entered it and how close he was...she could almost touch his towelling-clad shoulder if she reached out.

'Before I get in contact with the GMC I wanted to make certain that it's what you really want me to do,' he announced suddenly, catching her attention with a vengeance.

'Of course I do,' she said quickly, then added hesitantly, 'Unless *you're* having second thoughts about it?'

'Not in the least,' Josh said decisively, and from the way he said it she knew that he'd spent some considerable time thinking about this since they'd first discussed it yesterday.

Was this why he'd been so preoccupied yesterday evening? Because his mood hadn't changed much even when they'd had the good news about Mr Yandall.

'As you've been at pains to point out,' he continued briskly, 'I desperately need some assistance with the practice, especially while Tim's away. I can't wait until I can find a gold-plated locum, and I probably couldn't afford one, anyway.'

'Well, then…'

'Having said that,' he continued, fixing her with the full intensity of his dark blue gaze, 'if the GMC does sanction it I would like you to spend the rest of the time you're working with me seriously considering the possibility of becoming a GP registrar.'

'Oh, Josh, that's just what I—' she began, suddenly wanting to share her own deliberations with him—her realisation that she'd love to work for him and with him—but he had more to say.

'Not necessarily here,' he continued swiftly, as though concerned that she might feel pressurised into staying against her will. 'God knows we need more doctors in the area, but I honestly think you've got what it takes to make a damn good GP wherever you decide to practice.'

'Oh, Josh.' She smiled at the blunt compliment while her heart cracked a little. If he'd said that he wanted her to stay and work with him at Pendruccombe she'd have said yes like a shot. As it was, the idea of working so closely with anyone else…

'Thank you for the vote of confidence,' she said with a slightly shaky smile. 'Especially as it's a career possibility I hadn't even thought about before I came down here. When would you want to know my decision?'

'Well, I need to contact them as soon as their office is open this morning to regularise the situation here.' He flashed her a grin so full of charm and devilment that it nearly made her swallow her tongue. 'But be warned that when I speak to them I'll tell them I'm working on you!'

Bethan smiled, and turned to gaze out of her partially open curtains at the fresh new morning sky outside, as though considering what he'd said.

In reality, she was unable to bear looking at him while she was fighting the burning sensation in her eyes. She blinked twice and swallowed her disappointment, and the urge to cry began to recede.

'Was there anything else?' she prompted pleasantly when she turned back towards him, her cheeks beginning to ache with the effort of keeping her smile in place.

'Just that there's a possibility Phyllis might be able to fill in as a babysitter for Sam while Molly's away. I haven't asked her yet—I only thought about it a little while ago—but I remember her saying that she's at a loose end sometimes in the evenings and gets a bit lonely.'

'Well, if Laurence Foster is willing to fill in a bit more than usual, just until Tim returns from his honeymoon, it looks as if you've got the whole situation sorted out,' she said brightly. 'If that's what you wanted to tell me...?'

'Actually, there was one other thing,' he said, almost hesitantly, and this time he was the one avoiding her eyes.

Suddenly Bethan was intrigued, especially when she noticed that a tide of colour was sweeping up from the gaping neckline of his towelling wrap right up to his hairline.

'Is it something to do with your call to the GMC?' she prompted.

'No, it's more…personal.' Josh paused again and Bethan's curiosity began to grow in leaps and bounds.

'Well?'

'It's…' He paused again, then seemed to decide to spit it out and damn the consequences.

'I thought if I got up early this morning I could take my time in the bathroom without making anyone else late, but once I'd drawn the bath I realised that I wasn't going to be able to get in and out without risking another fall and…I wondered if…if you could…'

'Act as lifeguard?' she suggested lightly, and had to bite her tongue when she saw the expression of utter relief on his face because laughter bubbled so close to the surface.

'I'd be all right if it was *just* my knee or *just* my shoulder,' he said as he leant down to retrieve his crutches, 'but both together means that I can't hold my weight on either to get in and out.'

'You said you'd drawn the bath?' she asked as she reached for her own thin wrap and slid her arms into it, suddenly very conscious of the long length of leg visible beneath its short hem when she saw him looking at them.

'Have you got your clean clothes ready for afterwards?' she asked, trying to sound eminently practical.

'Yes, Mother,' he said with a rogue gleam in his eye, the first sign she'd had that he'd finally seen the humour in the situation.

Ever since they'd made love the two of them had been walking around each other as if on eggshells, hardly daring to go near each other in case they touched.

In spite of their precautions, each time their eyes met she felt her attraction towards him growing.

When she watched the care with which he looked after his patients, and the tenderness with which he treated his little daughter, she found herself wondering wistfully if she would ever have it directed towards her again.

When they'd made love everything had been too new for her to fully enjoy the pleasure. What would it be like now that she knew what to expect?

She remembered his gentle concern for her pleasure and the way he'd touched and praised her body, but what difference would it make to *Josh's* enjoyment if she was able to reciprocate properly when he—

'Bethan?'

His voice drew her out of her heated imaginings and she saw that he was already holding her door open.

'Coming,' she murmured, and sent up a silent prayer that she wasn't going to embarrass both of them.

She was tempted to peep when he undid the tie at the waist of his robe and slid it off his shoulders but she resisted, keeping her mind—and her eyes— strictly on the job as she helped him to balance as he climbed into the water.

She was even more severely tempted to openly ogle him when he propped his injured leg up on the side of the bath and lay back in the steaming depths with a groan of ecstasy, but forced herself to turn towards the basin to wash her face and brush her teeth.

There were intriguing splashing sounds behind her for several minutes then a couple of muted swear words before he spoke.

'Bethan? Could you…?'

'What?' She froze, sending a mental plea that whatever it was she would be able to control her wildly galloping hormones. How was she supposed to behave as if she was calmly unconcerned about being in here with him when all she wanted to do was ravish the man?

She almost turned to face him but remembered just in time to keep her eyes on the task of wringing out her flannel as if her life depended on it.

'I can't hang onto the grab rails to balance myself with my leg propped up there *and* wash my back at the same time,' he muttered, his deep voice more than a little exasperated.

When she realised what he was asking she squeezed her eyes tightly shut.

Damn, damn, double damn, two blasts, a hellfire and a bugger you... How did I ever get myself into this? she thought in despair, then straightened her shoulders and turned towards him.

'Scrubbing backs costs extra,' she warned lightly as she reached across him for the soap and flannel, keeping her eyes on her own hand rather than the long, lean, muscular, tanned—

'It'll be worth it, whatever you charge,' he said with feeling, snapping her out of the urge to salivate. 'I will be *so* glad when this knee's back to normal.'

As she opened the bathroom door Bethan was sure her face must still be pink after lathering and rinsing Josh's broad back. Her halo must have been shining, though, because in spite of the fact that the two of them were alone in such intimate proximity her eyes had never once strayed from their task.

Helping him out of the bath and into his towel had

been rather fraught because his skin was warm and slick with water, but they'd managed.

Bethan hadn't thought her pulse rate would ever go back to normal when she'd had to grab swiftly to stop his haphazardly wrapped towel from falling to the floor, but finally he was ready to make his way back to his room.

'Hello, Daddy. Hello, Bethan,' said Sam's chirpy voice from her bedroom door. 'What have you been doing?'

'G-good morning, sweetheart,' Bethan said, her mind totally blank for long seconds before it started functioning again. 'I was helping Daddy to have a bath.'

'Why? He can do it himself,' she said with a puzzled frown. 'He usually helps me.'

'Ah, but he can't manage at the moment with his knee all stiff,' Bethan explained, not daring to look towards Josh. 'He can't reach to scrub his back.'

'Ah.' The youngster smiled as if all was explained and Bethan heard Josh release a sigh of relief behind her.

Too soon.

'But...' Sam's frown was back. 'If you were helping him have a bath, what happened about washing...you know...' she glanced meaningfully towards her father's nether regions behind the towel '...his fuzzy bits.'

Behind her, Josh made a sound as if he were strangling and Bethan was hard put not to burst out laughing.

'Oh, that's no problem,' Bethan managed to say airily. 'He can reach those himself.'

'Oh, yes, of course,' Sam said with a nod, and turned back into her room. 'Is it nearly time for breakfast?'

CHAPTER NINE

'DAMN,' Josh muttered as he rolled over carefully and switched on the light.

He'd been staring at the ceiling ever since he'd gone to bed, his mind too full to allow him to sleep.

Now that Bethan had come in, he'd been listening to the sounds of her own preparations for bed with all the avidity of a teenager with his hormones on overload.

Where had she been this evening? Who had she met that she was home so late?

Home?

He chuckled softly, wryly. Who was he kidding? This wasn't Bethan's home, no matter how well she'd fitted in.

And she *did* fit in, as if she was meant to be here.

Sam loved her with all the emotion she'd been saving up in her heart since her mother had died. Even though he kept reminding her that Bethan would soon be going back to work, his stubborn little daughter had claimed Bethan as her own. He had a horrible feeling that she was going to be shattered when Bethan left.

And himself?

Josh drew in a deep breath and blew it out, feeling as if the sigh had come all the way from his soul. He had a similar horrible feeling that he wasn't going to be in a much better state than his daughter.

It had only been a week since she'd moved into the spare bedroom, and just five days since the GMC had given her assistance their blessing, but in a strange way it felt as if she'd been a part of their lives for ever.

With Molly away, and his own knee preventing him from moving easily, Bethan had taken over the more awkward jobs—like supervising Sam's bath—and it had done his heart good to hear the way the two of them splashed and laughed their way through the performance each evening.

This evening he'd been waiting on the edge of Sam's bed to read her the next chapter of her bedtime book when they'd come into the room.

Sam had looked freshly scrubbed and polished, with her dainty nightdress billowing around her legs as she straddled Bethan's hip, but it was *Bethan* he hadn't been able to take his eyes off.

Her eyes were shining and her cheeks pink despite the damp strands of hair, straggling onto her forehead and cheeks. She seemed to be carrying Sam awkwardly but it wasn't until he saw the way her wet T-shirt was plastered to her unfettered breasts that he realised that she was trying not to get Sam's nightdress wet.

She paused beside the bed but it wasn't until Josh heard her nervously clearing her throat that he looked up and realised that she had noticed where his eyes had been fastened.

He fought the guilty flush that climbed his cheeks but couldn't think of a single thing to say, his white-knuckled hands clutching the strategically placed book on his lap.

'Um… What time is Laurence due to arrive?' Bethan asked, and he couldn't help noticing that she was avoiding meeting his eyes as well.

He'd also noticed the way her nipples had hardened

into tightly furled buds under her T-shirt, and couldn't help remembering when he'd seen them naked...had held them in his hands and taken them in his mouth...

'Ah...any minute now,' he mumbled, dragging his thoughts back to her question. 'Calls permitting, he's going to stay for supper and a bit of socialising until about ten, then he'll go home and cover the rest of the night from there.'

'I don't *have* to go out tonight, you know,' she offered, seeming very earnest and, all of a sudden, very young and strangely unsure of herself. 'Phyllis was perfectly happy to stay over again to be here for Sam—especially now that we know about Peter—and you wouldn't have had to pay Laurence to cover.'

Bethan had been as delighted as if she had arranged the match herself to discover that Josh's other part-time receptionist, Phyllis, had just started going out with the paramedic she'd first met at the site of Josh's crash.

Peter Pemberthy was a widower with a couple of teenagers, while Phyllis had spent most of her adult life tied to a set of very demanding semi-invalid parents.

Since her mother had died eighteen months ago her responsibilities had ended and she'd taken a course as a medical receptionist.

Josh had met her when she'd started looking for jobs partway through her course and had been impressed with her professional attitude. He'd been equally delighted to find it was coupled with a similar share of motherly down-to-earth humanity and had hired her as soon as she'd finished her course. She'd been working for him ever since.

Her relationship with Peter was still very new and tentative, but Bethan had persuaded him to do what he could to give the two of them a nudge, by suggesting that Peter could keep her company in the evenings while Phyllis babysat for Sam.

'You *must* go out, even if it's only for a drink,' Josh had insisted, stamping down on the selfish thought that the evening was going to stretch out interminably until she returned. 'You've been here for a week and all you've done is work. It's supposed to be your holiday, for heaven's sake!'

Bethan had smiled and given in, but he thought she'd seemed strangely reluctant. Could it be that she actually enjoyed spending the time with him and his little daughter? He certainly knew that the two of them had been far happier since she'd come into their lives... In fact, Bethan was Sam's favourite topic of conversation.

Even when she wasn't around it was Bethan this and Bethan that.

And he was no better.

He'd spent the evening chatting idly to Laurence Foster while the older man verbally set the world to rights, but the whole time he'd been on edge, listening for the sound of her ridiculous Midgetmobile to return.

Now she was back, and as soon as he'd heard the sound of the shower being turned on all his senses had become painfully aroused.

It didn't matter that he tried to banish the image of her naked body slick with soapsuds and water, nor did clenching his hands into fists stop him remembering the way her silky smooth skin had felt when he'd stroked her.

The sound of Bethan brushing her teeth shouldn't have sounded sexy, but all he could think about was how fresh and minty her mouth would taste when he slid his tongue inside.

'Damn, damn, damn,' he muttered, and rolled over, then groaned when he landed on his bruised shoulder and gave his knee a wrench for good measure. At least the pain had taken his mind off making love to Bethan. Now maybe his arousal would recede enough to let him go to sleep.

He stared up at the ceiling and thought about the call-out they'd attended late this afternoon.

Bethan had been driving, although with the new articulated splint on his knee he was nearly mobile enough to start driving again—not that she would agree. Sometimes it almost seemed as if she was deliberately prolonging his dependence on her...

He slammed a lid on useless wishful thinking and pictured again the neglected garden surrounding the little cottage they'd been called to.

They couldn't really have missed it, with all the emergency vehicles parked outside.

'Can I help you, sir?' the young policeman had asked when Josh had rolled down the window.

'I'm Dr Kent. I understand there's a problem with one of my patients at this address?' Josh had said formally.

'Ah, yes, sir. If you'd like to park just beyond the ambulance...'

Peter Pemberthy had been waiting to speak to them when they'd climbed out, a unit of saline in one gloved hand and an unidentified package in the other.

'Hello, Josh, Bethan. Looks like an OD suicide,' he said briefly, his face drawn into serious lines as he led the way up the path and round to the back door.

'Luke Roseveare. He's...he *was* a relief milker at the farm. One of the neighbours came back from holiday late last night and heard the baby crying, and when it was still crying this afternoon went to knock to see if she could do anything to help. She knew that he'd lost his job a couple of weeks ago and then his girlfriend went off and left him with the baby.'

'And?' Josh's heart sank. He knew only too well what it felt like to be left with the awesome responsibility of taking care of a little child...how totally overwhelming it was to know that you were solely accountable for the child's welfare and happiness.

'The door wasn't locked so she stuck her head round and found him collapsed on the floor,' Peter continued. 'The babe was in his cot, hungry and dirty and very dehydrated. Could have been there for several days.'

'Poor scrap,' Josh said, his eyes already scanning the room as he stepped through the door, aware that Bethan was right behind him.

Part of him wanted to shield her from whatever they were about to see, but the more logical side knew that her training would have prepared her for such scenes.

'Ah, good,' said another voice, and when Josh's eyes grew accustomed to the dimness of the room after the bright sunlight outside he saw another policeman, straightening up from a crouch beside the body on the stretcher.

'Norman.' Josh greeted him with a nod. 'What have you got?'

'OD'd on veterinary drugs, by the look of it. The labs can soon tell us. He still had the syringe in his hand when he was found.'

'Shouldn't Forensics be here?' Josh said, aware that Bethan had quietly left the room as he leant forward to look at the face of the young man, recognising his painfully thin face and the long blond hair tied back into a ponytail with a piece of coloured yarn.

'Wouldn't want to do you out of a job,' the policeman said wryly. 'Needed you to be here for the baby, anyway, so while you're here I can get you to record the death and let the coroner sort the rest out. There's no sign of a struggle and nothing's been moved since he died. It's just another example of the idyllic life of the modern countryside—no job, no money, no hope…'

'How's the baby?' Josh asked when he'd finished the formalities.

'I understand they've got some fluids going into him, but I don't know much more. The bedroom's upstairs.'

Bethan was holding the child by the time he'd made his careful way up the steep stairs, and she'd looked up at him with eyes full of pain. He knew she was imagining the distress the little one must have been in, trapped in his cot in the airless bedroom with no one to change his nappy or give him a drink.

His eyes were sunken and his skin had taken on a strangely papery look, but at least the ambulancemen had been able to clean him up a bit and make him more comfortable.

He was such a tiny thing—about three months old, if Josh remembered correctly—and if the neighbour hadn't heard his cries when she had he would soon have been too weak to draw attention to himself…

'Are you all right?'

Bethan's soft voice dragged him back to the present with a jolt, and his eyes widened when he saw her standing just inside his room.

She was wearing a long nightdress, but with the

light on in the hallway behind her she might almost have been naked...

'I noticed your light on,' she whispered, and took another step towards him.

He nearly groaned aloud when his body was instantly fully aroused again. Dear God, what was the matter with him? It had never been like this for him before...had it?

Livvy had been his girlfriend through their last two years of school and the relationship had lasted right through their respective training until they could finally afford to marry.

Their relationship had grown and deepened over the years, and while there had been no bells and whistles their sex life had been comfortable and satisfying.

As far as he knew, they'd both been totally faithful to each other, and until he'd met Bethan a week ago he hadn't even been interested in going to bed with another woman. It had been enough for him to simply make it to the end of each day.

Now all he had to do was catch a lingering trace of the scent of her soap, or hear her laughter when she was playing with Sam, and all he could think about was burying himself up to the hilt in her and staying there until the world came to an end.

'I couldn't sleep,' he said, all too aware that his voice was husky with arousal. 'I was thinking about—' About you...about your perfect body...about the way you've brought sunshine into all the dark corners of my life...about the way I want to wrap you in my arms and never let you go. 'About the baby.'

'Oh, Josh,' Bethan breathed as she flew on silent feet towards him. 'I've been thinking about him all evening. Have you heard anything?'

She perched herself on the side of his bed and thought she heard him groan.

'I'm sorry, did I hurt your knee?' She turned and reached out towards his leg under the bedclothes.

'No!' he said with a strange degree of urgency in his voice. 'It's fine… You didn't hurt it.'

'Well?' she demanded eagerly. 'How's the baby?'

'He's doing well. So well, in fact, that he's demanding real food already—at least, a bottle!'

'What about his family?' she asked. 'Have they been able to find out whether he's got anyone?'

'The police are trying to trace his mother, but in view of the fact that she'd abandoned him with his father he'll probably be placed in care.'

'Poor little scrap. Do they think he's going to be all right?'

'As far as they can tell, he shouldn't suffer from any long-term ill-effects.'

She sighed with relief. 'I was telling Jane about him this evening.'

'Jane?' he frowned. He couldn't think whom she might have met since she'd been staying at Pendruccombe…

'Jane Trethorne—the nurse at the show who trained at the same hospital?' she reminded him.

'Fancy meeting up with her again. What a coincidence!'

'Actually, she told me that a group of them meet up every so often for a drink and an evening of letting their hair down. It can be difficult sometimes, socialising with people who don't have a medical background, so they've devised this unofficial ''club''. They all get a chance to tell grisly jokes and swap notes about what's going on in their particular field.'

'Such as?'

He leant back into the pile of pillows against his headboard and Bethan was pleased to see that he seemed to be more relaxed than when she'd first sat down beside him.

'Such as... I told them how surprised I was that people would risk their lives, messing about with veterinary drugs, and one of the group was a vet who told me that abuse of veterinary drugs is absolutely rampant. Apparently they now have just as many drugs-related break-ins as doctors' surgeries or pharmacists.'

'I hadn't realised that the situation had got quite that bad,' Josh said with a frown. 'I know we had to put in some fairly hefty bars and locks for our little supply of drugs—the insurance company insisted on it. It's interesting to hear that other similar professions are in the same boat. Did you hear any other snippets?'

'Not really, except Jane was telling me about Kernowdoc.'

'Ah,' Josh murmured.

'So you *do* know about the organisation?' she said.

'Of course. I could hardly be in practice in Cornwall *without* knowing,' he confirmed. 'The last time I looked at the figures I think it was two-thirds of all the GPs had joined.'

'Well, why haven't you?' Bethan demanded. 'It's absolutely ideal for small practices like yours. Instead of having to be on call every second or third night and every second or third weekend—when you're all here—you could be covering just four or five duties in a month!'

'Do you think I don't *know* that?' he demanded, and for the first time she could hear the frustration in his voice. 'I thought it was a marvellous idea right from the first, but Martin was dead set against it.'

'For heaven's sake, why? Was he a glutton for punishment? Did he *like* working day after day on insufficient sleep?'

'Obviously not, bearing in mind that the stress has contributed to his becoming an alcoholic,' Josh commented wryly. 'He wasn't so bad when Pam was alive, but she died of ovarian cancer about eighteen months ago and he hasn't been quite right ever since.'

'Then why?' she persisted. 'Is he trying to make certain that you have a breakdown, too?'

'Hardly,' he snorted. 'It's more a case of wanting to cling to the system he knows—the one that preserves the continuity of care for the patients. He's afraid that people will slip through the cracks if patients see a different doctor every time.'

'But that's not the way it works,' she objected. 'Jane explained that if someone phones after surgery hours their call goes to a central control where a doctor can talk to them to decide how urgent their situation is.

'He'll talk to them and decide whether they need a home visit, whether they are well enough to get themselves to a regional centre such as the local hospital or whether they can wait to see their GP in the morning. Then the next morning a copy of all the paperwork goes to the patient's own GP for their file.'

'I know,' Josh said tiredly. 'They're using the modern technology of computers and faxes to speed the delivery of care to the patients while we're little better than the horse and cart.

'Urgent cases are faxed straight through to the patient's own GP by the control centre if necessary, while time-wasters are weeded out right from the first phone call.

'You wouldn't believe how frustrating it's been for us, knowing that we've been driving all over the countryside every other night while the GPs who *have* joined have a driver provided to get them from one centre to the other, with only the odd trips to the patient's own home.'

'So, if you and Tim both think it's a good idea, why don't you join? It's been running long enough for the initial rough spots to be ironed out.'

'Martin's the senior partner by virtue of the number of years he's been working in the practice, and he's dead set against it,' Josh reminded her.

'But he's not even working here any more,' she pointed out bluntly. 'And, from what I understand, he's unlikely to be able to cope with coming back to work while the pressure continues at this level. Apart from that, have you ever thought that the fact you're *not* part of Kernowdoc might be one of the reasons why you can't get another doctor to join you to take part of the load off you?'

'Catch twenty-two,' he said wryly. 'Damned if we do and damned if we don't.'

'I can think of one person who would definitely welcome the change if you did,' Bethan added softly. 'It would certainly mean you had more time for Sam—time when you weren't too exhausted to go out and do things together.'

'Oh, very sneaky,' he murmured. 'You know how to go for the jugular, don't you?'

'But I've given you something to think about?' she prompted. 'Surely it would be worth tackling Martin again and giving him an honest picture of how the practice, and the doctors in particular, are suffering because of his initial prejudice?'

'After this last fiasco I shall definitely sit down for a long chat with Tim as soon as he gets back.'

'I can't see that he'd object to spending more time with his new wife,' Bethan pointed out.

'You're right,' he grinned. 'Perhaps Tim should take her with us when we go to tackle Martin.' His smile died as he paused thoughtfully. 'Would it make a difference to you?' he asked softly.

'To me?' She was puzzled.

'To whether you decided to become a GP registrar?' he explained. 'Would you be more likely to want to join a practice that was part of Kernowdoc than one that wasn't?'

'It's certainly a point to consider. I don't think many doctors would willingly join a practice where they were going to be putting themselves through those ghastly years of training—working over a hundred hours a week for months on end—with no end in sight.'

She hoped her voice had sounded noncommittal enough that he wouldn't see the real answer in her eyes—that she wouldn't really care either way as long as the practice had one Dr Joshua Kent in it.

'Josh? I've been thinking,' Bethan said several days later as she stood in front of the mirror in the bathroom, practising her little speech before she went down to the sitting room and delivered it in person.

'Tim's due back at the end of the week, and I've actually got another week's holiday due to me. I know your knee is much better, but would it be an idea if I stayed just a bit longer to...?'

She drew in a deep breath and blew it out very slowly.

'No chance,' she muttered. 'He's certainly recovered enough to be able to drive himself again and, with Molly back, I'm just a spare part in a well-oiled machine.'

She pulled a face at herself in the mirror and collected her wash kit up, knowing that the only reason she wanted to stay was to be close to Josh.

Oh, he'd been the perfect gentleman.

Since that first night he'd hardly touched her—even to pass her a cup of coffee—and she was running out of time.

She'd been so certain that there was a special spark between them, something she could fan into a lasting flame that the two of them could warm themselves by for a lifetime together. Now she was wondering if it had all been wishful thinking.

Her own love wasn't in doubt. She knew that she'd fallen in love with Josh but without some sign from him she had no idea if it was reciprocated.

Hence the last-ditch attempt to prolong their time together...

'It's either that or I cut my losses,' she said finally as she flicked the lock and opened the door.

'Oh, it's just you,' said Sam as she craned her head round into the bathroom. 'I heard you talking and I thought you were giving Daddy another bath.'

'No, Sam, I was just talking to myself,' Bethan said as she felt the heat crawl up her cheeks. 'Perhaps I'm getting old.'

'Are you *very* old?' she quizzed. 'I'm going to be five in September. I've got it on my calendar. Do you want to see?'

Bethan followed the little sprite, delighted to see

her able to walk without crutches now she'd been given the all-clear and glad that the topic of her father's bath had been abandoned.

'See. There it is. The big red number.' She pointed gleefully to the hand-made chart on the door of her wardrobe. 'Anna made it for me this morning so I can count the days to *my* birthday and *Daddy's* birthday.' She put another finger on the second red number just next door. 'I've got a crayon to colour each day when it's gone.'

'You and your daddy have birthdays on next-door days?' Bethan asked, making sure of her facts.

'Yes. He said I was his best birthday present, but I arrived in the post one day too soon.'

'Well, if I were his present, I would have arrived one day too late because *my* birthday is the day *after* his,' Bethan said, thoroughly enjoying Sam's delight.

'Now we can share our birthday with you too,' she announced. 'Daddy and me put all our candles on one big cake and I help him to blow his out.'

Bethan smiled. It was so long since she'd bothered to celebrate her birthday in late September, so long since she'd had anyone who wanted to celebrate it with her. The idea of a joint birthday with her two favourite people in the whole world was unbearably sweet, especially as she would be far away.

'Why do you look sad?' Sam said, tugging on Bethan's hand to pull her back down. 'Don't you want to share our birthday?'

'I'd love to share it, Sam, but I'll be back at work again by then,' she explained gently. 'Back at the hospital.'

'But you can work here, then you wouldn't have to go back,' Sam said with perfect logic. 'Then you could share.'

If only it were that simple, Bethan thought. To simply rearrange her life so that she could be here to share her birthday with this lively little imp.

Why not? whispered the seductive voice in the back of her mind. You could arrange to have a long weekend off... You'd be able to see Sam again...and Josh...

CHAPTER TEN

'MIDGETMOBILE,' Bethan muttered, and slapped her hand on the steering-wheel. 'I could think of something far more appropriate for you at the moment, you rotten old bucket of rust. Why did you have to give up the ghost *today* of all days?'

Something caught her eye in the mirror and she looked up in time to see the rescue vehicle pull in behind her, his warning lights flashing.

The mechanic had more hair on his chin than on his head, and *that* was an unusual shade of marmalade streaked with grey, but he couldn't have been more friendly or helpful.

'Going somewhere special?' he asked chattily as he prepared to replace the fanbelt in her engine.

'A birthday party, if I'm not too late,' Bethan said with another glance at her watch.

'You'll be there in plenty of time,' he reassured her. 'What time does it start? Seven? Eight?'

'I'm not sure. She's going to be five, but I don't know whether it'll be a tea-party or something later.' Bethan bit her lip, wondering if she was making a gigantic mistake.

It had been just over a month since she'd left Pendruccombe, leaving a tearful Sam with the promise that she would return to share her birthday, but in spite of leaving that letter for Josh she hadn't heard a word from him.

In the end she'd decided that, whether he liked it or not, she *was* going to be there for Sam. She was going to keep her promise, even if she had to find herself accommodation for the night afterwards.

She closed her eyes as she relived for the millionth time the phone call that had spelled the end of her time with Josh.

It had been her own idea to see if she could extend her stay in Cornwall, knowing that she'd still had some days of holiday owing to her.

She'd waited, having decided to make her phone call when Josh took the car out alone for the first time since his accident. Her intention had been to surprise him with a *fait accompli* when he came back, and she'd hoped that springing the idea on him like that would startle him into showing what her presence meant to him—whether there was any hope that his feelings would one day match hers.

What she hadn't been prepared to hear when she got through to the hospital was that Simon had just accepted a plum job at another hospital and wanted to be released as soon as possible, and that the registrar had broken his arm windsurfing.

'I can't possibly give you permission to extend your holiday,' said the voice on the other end of the phone, sounding close to panic. 'In fact, if you could return immediately I'll make certain that you receive extra days off in compensation later.'

'But—' *Later* wouldn't be the same. It was here and now that mattered.

'We're desperate, Dr Mallory. You know as well as I do that we were already running short-handed in the department, but now...'

Bethan knew she had no real option...not if she was going to be able to live with herself. Honesty forced her to admit that Josh didn't *really* need her help any more, and Molly was already back to look after Sam...

One corner of her mind was registering the sounds of the mechanic, clattering about under the hood of her car, while the rest was remembering the way she'd flung her belongings in her cases and carried them out to her car.

All the time she'd been keeping an eye out for Josh to return, knowing that he could be several hours yet, she'd been cursing herself for being greedy.

If she hadn't wanted to stay on for just a few more days with Josh she wouldn't have phoned the hospital, and then she wouldn't have known that they'd needed her. She could have stayed to the end of her allotted time with a clear conscience...

Sam had trailed backwards and forwards behind Bethan like her little shadow, with her bedraggled lamb clutched in her arms and silent tears trickling down her face.

Even a promise that she would return to share her birthday hadn't been able to pacify the little girl so Bethan had spared the time to go through to Josh's consulting room to sit down at his desk one last time and write her promise down in a letter.

'I've done one for you and one for your daddy,' she said, holding up the two sheets of paper.

'The birthday promise?' Sam said, and sniffed pathetically.

'The birthday promise,' Bethan agreed, utterly determined that unless Josh contacted her to tell her he didn't want her to come she would keep it.

'Will you put them in an envelope so I can keep them safe, like Daddy does?' Sam said.

Bethan smiled and took an envelope out of Josh's desk to slide the letters in.

'There you are. Now you can keep it safe. That's to tell you that I'll be there for your birthday,' she repeated, and hugged the precious youngster to her one last time.

She'd had to hurry out then, with scant farewells for Anna and Molly, before her own tears started to fall.

It had been a long lonely month waiting for 'Septober' to come. Days of missing Josh's company and Sam's hugs, nights of lying awake and wishing, then falling asleep and dreaming.

Now she was nearly there...would already *be* there if the car hadn't died on her...

'There you go!' said a cheerful voice, and the mechanic emerged, wiping his greasy hands on an equally greasy rag. 'That shouldn't give you any more trouble. You'll be able to get to where you're going. Ask your usual mechanic to check it over next time you take the car in, just in case the tension needs adjusting.'

Bethan signed his paperwork in a fever of anxiety to be gone.

Now that she'd got so far she resented anything that held her up. The answer to her future, one way or another, lay just a bit further along the road at Pendruccombe.

'Are you ready to light the candles on the cake, Sam?' Josh said persuasively, but his little daughter just shook her head, her nose almost glued to the window where she'd been waiting almost all afternoon.

She was wearing her new dress in honour of the day and, for the first time that he could remember, actually looked more like Samantha than Sam.

He'd realised at the time that she'd been getting too attached to Bethan during the short time she'd been with them…he'd had exactly the same problem…but his daughter's stubborn persistence that Bethan had promised to share her birthday was breaking his heart.

She'd even refused to let him invite any of her friends from her playschool group so there was no frantic noise and laughter to take her mind off the fact that Bethan wasn't coming.

'I'll phone the hospital so you can talk to her, shall I?' he offered, hoping that idea would spark her interest, but she'd shaken her head.

'She won't be there,' Sam said, sticking out her stubborn little chin and turning back to lean her little elbows on the windowsill while she gazed out towards the road. 'She's coming here in her car to share our birthday. She promised.'

'I'm sorry, but Dr Mallory is not available. Can I get someone else to help you?' said the voice on the other end of the phone when desperation forced Josh to try anyway.

'I need to get in contact with her urgently. Have you got another number for her?' he asked persuasively.

'If I may explain,' he began again. 'She did a locum for me while I was injured, and there's a child with a heart condition who needs to speak to her…' Well, Sam was sick at heart…missing Bethan as much as she'd ever missed her own mother, he told himself in justification for stretching the truth so far.

'I'm sorry, but you have to understand that it's not hospital policy to give out staff telephone numbers,' the disembodied voice repeated patiently. 'If you could leave your own name and number I'll try to make sure that she gets it as soon as possible.'

He left a message then put the phone down to wander slowly through to the sitting room where Sam was still keeping her vigil.

'Damn, damn, damn,' he muttered, and even that reminded him of Bethan and her grandmother's litany.

Wretched woman—if he had her here in front of him he'd throttle her for turning the two of them inside out.

If only he'd followed the prompting of his heart and had tried to contact Bethan as soon as she'd left…but the way she'd done it had seemed so utterly final.

A great wave of sadness engulfed Josh as he remembered how he'd felt when he'd returned home to find Sam crying and almost incoherent and Bethan gone without a word.

Molly hadn't been much help, going round with a long face muttering dire fragments.

'Said she couldn't live with herself if she didn't go straight away,' was one often-repeated refrain, the one that made his heart feel as if it had been removed on the end of a rusty skewer.

If he'd thought Sam had reacted badly when Bethan had first left, he had an idea that it would be nothing to her crushing disappointment when Bethan didn't turn up as promised for her birthday.

He slumped into his favourite chair and leant his head back wearily as he contemplated the last month.

For all the extra sleep he was getting, he and Tim might just as well not have decided to face Martin down with a demand that he agree to join Kernowdoc.

At least Tim was reaping the benefit now that they were working a more reasonable set of hours, with plenty of time to help Leanne with the remodelling of the old cottage they'd bought out on the edge of Tresillet.

If he hadn't been such a good friend over the last couple of years Josh could almost have been jealous of the love the two newly-weds shared, their every gesture and look a testament to the deep emotion—

'She's here!' shrieked Sam suddenly, shocking him out of his grim thoughts as she started jumping up and down in her excitement. 'Bethan's here!'

She took off at a run towards the door, pausing only long enough to beam triumphantly back at him. 'See! I told you she would... She promised!' And she was gone in a thunder of little running feet.

'She's here!' Bethan heard from somewhere inside the house in front of her and her heart rose. At least she knew that *Sam* was pleased to see her...had apparently remembered her promise and had been waiting for her to arrive.

'Oh, Bethan, you came!' said a happy voice as the door was flung open and a little body flung itself into her arms.

'Sweetheart!' Bethan caught her and wrapped the child tightly in her arms, squeezing her eyes shut as she relished the precious feel of this little girl who had such a tight hold on her heart.

'Bethan,' said a deep voice, and her pulse hammered as she looked all the way up into familiar deep blue eyes in a strangely shuttered face.

'Josh,' she breathed, knowing that she was devouring him with her eyes and horribly afraid that her every emotion would be there for him to see.

It felt like an aeon since she'd left Pendruccombe and it wasn't until she'd seen Josh that she'd realised she'd never be able to leave again because her heart belonged here with him.

'Would you like to come in?' he said politely, as if she were little more than a stranger. 'Apparently, you've been invited to join our birthday party.'

'*Share*, Daddy,' Sam said firmly, lifting her head from Bethan's shoulder just long enough to correct him before she wrapped her arms around Bethan's neck again.

Bethan straightened and had taken the first step towards him when she stopped.

'Oh! I nearly forgot,' she said. 'I've left your presents in the car.'

'I already got my birthday promise,' Sam said. 'I kept it safe for my birthday, just like you said. Shall I show you?'

Bethan wasn't quite sure what she was talking about, but when the little girl wriggled she put her down and watched her run inside, marvelling at how beautiful she was, how tall she had grown in just a month, and her leg... She didn't even seem to have a limp any more...

'I'll just...' Bethan turned towards Josh and her throat closed up when she saw that he had been watching her, his face still strangely devoid of expression. She'd hoped that he'd just been discreet while Sam was around, had hoped deep in her heart that he would welcome her with open arms and a declaration of love, but they were alone now and he didn't look as if he had anything to say to her at all.

She whirled and took the few steps to her car—the Midgetmobile, as she'd begun calling it after Josh's derogatory comment so long ago—and reached inside for the parcels she'd brought with her.

'You shouldn't have bothered,' he said quietly be-

hind her, and she jumped. She hadn't realised that
he'd followed her across to the car, his big body
looming over her.

'It was no bother. I enjoyed choosing—'

'She was just starting to get over you,' he interrupted angrily, his impassivity completely gone as his
deep blue eyes blazed at her and his hands clenched
as if he was imagining them around her neck. 'Now
she'll have to go through it all over again.'

Bethan was struck speechless. She'd imagined all
sorts of receptions but not this barely leashed fury. If
he had been so adamantly against her coming, why
hadn't he contacted her and told her so?

She'd given him her phone number in the letter
she'd left with Sam, hoping that she would hear from
him—hoping he'd use it to tell her that he missed her
and wanted her to come back to him.

If he'd rung her to tell her not to come today it
would have hurt…it would have felt as if he had
ripped her heart out by the roots…but she would have
abided by his wishes and spoken to Sam with an excuse.

But to ignore her unspoken message, to leave
everything in limbo for a month without a word…

'Here it is, Bethan. Look!'

Sam appeared in the doorway, waving an envelope,
her bright happiness piercing the suffocating cloud
hanging over the two adults.

'What have you got there, sweetheart?' Bethan
asked, crouching down to look.

'It's the envelope you put my promise in,' she said
importantly. 'You told me it was the promise for my
birthday and I kept it till you came.'

Bethan drew in a sharp breath and glanced in horror
from the envelope to Josh and back.

'Is… Is your daddy's letter in there too?' she asked faintly as her pulse hammered so hard in her chest that it was an effort to force air into her lungs.

'Yes. Look. I kept his promise safe too,' she said proudly. 'Do you want it now?' she asked her father, smiling up at him guilelessly. 'Bethan gave it to me to look after for you. I was crying when she had to go back to work so she wrote a promise for me and a promise for you and put them in here.'

Clumsily she untucked the flap Bethan had tucked in for her and chubby little fingers fished inside for the two pieces of paper Bethan had put there a month ago.

'Is this my one?' Sam demanded as she handed the first one to her father, hopping from one foot to the other in anticipation.

Josh gazed from the single sheet up to Bethan and back again before he unfolded it, an arrested expression on his face.

'Yes, Sam, it's yours,' he said in a husky voice, and bent down beside her to show her, his finger following the words the way it did when he read her stories at bedtime.

'It says, "Dear Sam-antha, I love you very much and I promise that I will come to share your birthday in September." And it's signed, "Bethan".'

'See!' she crowed triumphantly, wriggling like a little puppy inside his encircling arm as she took the paper back from him and started to try to slide it back inside the envelope. 'I told you she promised!'

Josh glanced up at Bethan again before he cleared his throat, and she saw his chest expand as he drew in a deep breath.

'Sam, have you still got *my* letter in your envelope?' he asked huskily, and held his hand out.

Bethan had to bite her lip when she saw the fine tremor in his hand as Sam reverently placed the second sheet of paper in it.

'Read it, Daddy,' she demanded. 'What does it say?'

The seconds stretched out interminably as Bethan watched Josh's eyes scan the handful of lines she'd written in such haste. She barely remembered what she'd written...other than the fact that she'd poured her heart out to him.

'Well?' Sam said impatiently, bouncing up and down beside him. 'What does yours say?'

'It says the same as yours,' Josh said in a voice thickened by emotion as he gazed up at Bethan. 'It says, "Dear Josh, I love you very much and I promise to come and share your birthday in Septober." And it's signed, "Love, Bethan".'

'Near enough,' Bethan whispered as her heart seemed to swell to fill her chest and her eyes burned with happy tears. 'Except you forgot the last line. "Please can I stay until your next birthday and the one after that and the one after...?"' her voice failed her.

'That's the thing about people who share birthdays in Septober,' he said huskily, his deep blue eyes fixed on her with gleaming intensity as he straightened with Sam in his arms and walked towards her. 'Once you've shared one you get to share the rest of them for ever.' He wrapped his free arm around her to bring her into their circle.

'Has the post arrived yet?' Bethan demanded as Josh tried to hurry her out of the door.

'I don't know, and we haven't got time to find out,' Josh said impatiently, with one hand at her back and the suitcase in his hand. 'The car's ready outside the door. It's going to take us half an hour to get there—more, if there are any delays.'

'But I don't want to go without finding out,' she said stubbornly. 'If it's arrived I want to see it with my own eyes.'

'Bethan...'

'Please, Josh?' She gazed up at him, knowing that where she and Sam were concerned he really *was* as soft as butter.

'All right!' Exasperation filled his voice. 'I'll go and find out while you get into the car. Here are the keys. Bethan...!'

She was already on her way down the corridor towards the practice, determined that if the envelope had arrived she was going to be there to see it opened.

It wasn't that she was in any doubt that she'd passed her year as a GP registrar successfully—with Josh as her mentor how could she have done otherwise? It was just that she really wanted the satisfaction of closing one chapter in her life before she opened the first page of the next one.

'Hello, Phyllis,' she said with a warm smile for the newly married woman. 'I can see from the glow on your face that you and Peter had a wonderful honeymoon. Is the post here yet?'

'Arrived about ten minutes ago,' Phyllis said with a grin and a soft blush. 'And, yes, it was wonderful.'

She reached for the thick bundle held together with an elastic band, knowing what Bethan was waiting for.

Bethan was so impatient to see if her envelope was there that she was tempted to snatch the whole bundle out of Phyllis's hands, but she concentrated on controlling her breathing while she watched her flick through the pile.

'No, no, no... Yes!' she said, and plucked one out of the middle to hand it over. 'Do you want the letter-opener?'

'Too late!' Bethan said with a grin as she slid a fingernail under the edge of the flap and ripped it open with a flourish. 'Yes!' she said triumphantly.

'Are you happy now?' Josh demanded with an exasperated hand on each hip.

'Yes! Yes! Yes!' Bethan sang, and waved the paper in the air as she twirled round in a circle. 'It's official. I'm no longer a registrar, I'm a GP!'

'I'll tell you what you are,' Josh said grimly as he grabbed one hand and dragged her across the room in his wake. 'You're a very *pregnant* GP who's been in labour long enough to send me completely grey. Now, will you *please* get in the car so I can take you to the hospital?'

'There's no rush, you know,' Bethan said calmly as he helped her into the seat as though she were a priceless piece of china. 'The baby won't be arriving for hours yet. There's plenty of time.'

'I know you did a six-month stint on Obs and Gyn,' he said, then swore under his breath when he realised that he was trying to put the front door key into the car ignition. 'But that should have been enough to tell you that even though first babies are often late there's no guarantee of it so we're getting to the hospital in plenty of time.'

'There's plenty of time, I tell you,' Bethan said as she settled back in her seat. 'Even time enough for you to go back in the house and fetch the suitcase that you put down in the hall...'

Josh groaned and rested his forehead on the steering-wheel.

'I thought life was exhausting *before* I met you,' he muttered, then released his seat belt and trudged back to get the case.

'Oh, Josh, I do love you,' Bethan said, just before the next contraction began to grip her in its jaws. 'But, really, you can take the journey slowly, I promise.'

'What makes you so certain?' Josh asked, taking his eyes off the road ahead just long enough to flick a glance at his watch that told Bethan he was keeping count of the diminishing number of minutes between contractions.

'Didn't Sam tell you?' Bethan said when she got her breath back. 'She's already had a long discussion with the baby and told it all about sharing birthdays, and she told it quite categorically that she wanted a baby as a birthday present.'

'And you actually believe that this baby is going to wait to arrive to order?'

'Why not?' Bethan said with a wicked grin. 'It was virtually started to order...'

'Bethan,' he growled, and she giggled when she saw the way his neck grew red.

'Sam said that we'd been married a long time—'

'Three months!' he interrupted.

'And she thought it was about time we did something about getting her a baby brother or sister.'

'It was Phyllis's and Anna's idea to send us on that belated honeymoon,' he pointed out.

'Well, your knee was still a little fragile when we first got married for you to have been as...energetic...as you were that week!'

'As energetic as *we* were,' Josh corrected huskily.

'And please don't remind me that there's another six weeks before we can—'

'Be "energetic" again?' she suggested.

'Behave yourself, woman,' he growled as he pulled up outside the hospital entrance closest to the maternity unit and hurried round to help her out of the car. 'I don't want to be walking in there with my wife in labour and my—'

'Hormones showing?' she teased as the automatic doors slid open in front of them, then gasped and gripped his hand tight, almost doubled over by the force of the next contraction.

'Won't arrive till tomorrow, eh?' he mocked as he grabbed the wheelchair, rushed across to him by a porter. 'I've a feeling that this little one has decided to do the same to Sam as *she* did to me—her birthday present's going to arrive one day early.'

'Told you so,' Josh said, sounding impossibly smug as Bethan gazed down at the dark-haired bundle in her arms.

'Only by half an hour,' she pointed out petulantly. 'When everything went off the boil when we got to the labour ward I was certain that Sam was going to get her wish.'

'Well, I certainly got all my wishes,' he said as he perched on the edge of the bed and slid one arm around her. 'One ordeal over, one wife healthy and happy and one baby delivered safely. Now all we've got to do is decide on a name.'

The baby in her arms stretched and opened dark eyes to gaze up at them...so dark that there was no way of telling yet whether they were going to be blue or brown.

'Actually, I'd thought of Samuel,' Bethan suggested, tongue in cheek. 'If it was shortened to Sam then everyone would *know* that we've got double trouble. The only problem is—what would we call the next one?'

'Oh, I'm sure we'll think of something,' Josh said with a chuckle. 'After all, we've got plenty of time.'

'All the time in the world,' Bethan agreed as she stroked one hand over her little son's head then turned her face up to receive Josh's kiss.

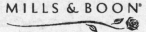

MILLS & BOON

Emma Darcy

The Collection

❋ ❋ ❋ ❋

This autumn Mills & Boon® brings you a powerful
collection of three full-length novels by an
outstanding romance author:

Always Love
To Tame a Wild Heart
The Seduction of Keira

Over 500 pages of love, seduction and intrigue.

Available from September 1998

*Available at most branches of WH Smith, John Menzies,
Martins, Tesco, Asda, and Volume One*

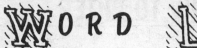ORD INK

We are giving away a year's supply of Mills & Boon® books to the five lucky winners of our latest competition. Simply fill in the ten missing words below, complete the coupon overleaf and send this entire page to us by 28th February 1999. The first five correct entries will each win a year's subscription to the Mills & Boon series of their choice. What could be easier?

BUSINESS	__SUIT__	CASE
BOTTLE	_____	HAT
FRONT	_____	BELL
PARTY	_____	BOX
SHOE	_____	PIPE
RAIN	_____	TIE
ARM	_____	MAN
SIDE	_____	ROOM
BEACH	_____	GOWN
FOOT	_____	KIND
BIRTHDAY	_____	BOARD

Please turn over for details of how to enter ⇨

C8H

HOW TO ENTER

There are ten words missing from our list overleaf. Each of the missing words must link up with the two on either side to make a new word or words.

For example, 'Business' links with 'Suit' and 'Case' to form 'Business Suit' and 'Suit Case':

$$\text{BUSINESS—SUIT—CASE}$$

As you find each one, write it in the space provided. When you have linked up all the words, fill in the coupon below, pop this page into an envelope and post it today. Don't forget you could win a year's supply of Mills & Boon® books—you don't even need to pay for a stamp!

Mills & Boon Word Link Competition
FREEPOST CN81, Croydon, Surrey, CR9 3WZ

EIRE readers: (please affix stamp) PO Box 4546, Dublin 24.

Please tick the series you would like to receive if you are one of the lucky winners

Presents™ ❑   Enchanted™ ❑   Medical Romance™ ❑
Historical Romance™ ❑   Temptation®

Are you a Reader Service™ subscriber?   Yes ❑   No ❑

Ms/Mrs/Miss/Mr ....Initials..........................
(BLOCK CAPITALS PLEASE)

Surname..

Address ....

....

....Postcode..........................

(I am over 18 years of age)   C8H